Dedications

To my parents and to my wonderful illustrator and publisher. Your enthusiasm and support are more valuable than all the treasure in the world!

Sophia Slewfoot Solves
The Mystery of the
Oak Island Treasure
History's Mysteries

Marie-Louise Gregory

Illustrated by Nicola Brooks

A CIP catalogue record for this title is available from the
British Library.

ISBN 978-1-7398655-3-5 (Paperback)

2 4 6 8 10 9 7 5 3 1

First published 2022

Muddy Publishing Ltd
www.muddypublishing.com

Chapter 1

Sophia Slewfoot was an ordinary ten year old girl, but today was not an ordinary day.

Today, for the first time ever, Sophia was going to take her best friend, Betty Babbington, on a real life, time-travelling, history's mystery-solving adventure.

That's right! An actual real life adventure that would involve travelling through time, and maybe even across the world, to some far away time and place. A time and place where one of history's great mysteries was unfolding, ready to be resolved by Sophia and Betty. The girls were two brave, budding amateur detectives who loved history and who really, really loved solving mysteries.

Even though she didn't know yet what the adventure would be, or where or when it would take them, Sophia knew that the day ahead would be one of the most exciting of her life!

Now, those readers who have not yet met Sophia Slewfoot and Betty Babbington will probably be asking themselves how on earth Sophia could know that the day ahead of her would involve a time-travelling, history's mystery-solving adventure. After all, how can anyone know anything about the future, and how can anyone possibly have an adventure in the past?

The answers to these questions arise from the fact that, a short while ago, Sophia Slewfoot and her family had moved into a new (but nearly 300 year old) house in a small village in the North West of England. On her first day exploring her new home Sophia had happened upon a hidden doorway that was papered over and concealed in the landing wall. Behind the hidden doorway, Sophia had discovered a secret staircase. She had braved the dark and the dusty cobwebs and she had climbed the spiral stairs to find an ancient hidey-hole room. In the room and camouflaged by its red, crumbling bricks, was an old, rusty safe. Sophia had managed to unlock the safe using a beautifully intricate and ornate key which had lain, for years and years, under an old floorboard, until Sophia's dog, a lovely Beagle named Toby, had cleverly sniffed it out. Stored away inside the safe, was something very, very special and very, very secret.

The very, very special and very, very secret something was Sophia's 'PT machine'. Short for planisphera temporalabe[1], the machine resembled, at first glance, an old-fashioned carriage clock that could have held pride of place on a grand Victorian mantelpiece. However,

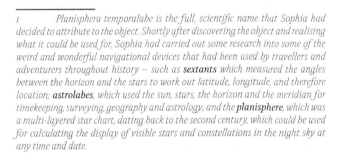

---

[1]   *Planisphera temporalabe is the full, scientific name that Sophia had decided to attribute to the object. Shortly after discovering the object and realising what it could be used for, Sophia had carried out some research into some of the weird and wonderful navigational devices that had been used by travellers and adventurers throughout history – such as* **sextants** *which measured the angles between the horizon and the stars to work out latitude, longitude, and therefore location;* **astrolabes***, which used the sun, stars, the horizon and the meridian for timekeeping, surveying, geography and astrology; and the* **planisphere***, which was a multi-layered star chart, dating back to the second century, which could be used for calculating the display of visible stars and constellations in the night sky at any time and date.*

Sextant

Astrolabe

Planisphere

despite appearances, the machine was not just some old clock. Oh no!

The PT machine was made of what must have been real gold, as the object had been locked away for many years, but it was shiny and beautiful and not tarnished at all. The 'clock' face was made of a creamy, shimmering mother-of-pearl, which seemed to glow, even in the tiny, windowless, hidey-hole room. Running around the edge of the face, in Roman numerals fashioned from onyx (a black precious stone), were the numbers 1 to 12, just like you would find on an ordinary clock. That, though, was where the similarities to a clock came to an end.

Running around the circular rim of the object, outside the mother-of-pearl face, and etched into the gold itself, were inscriptions which Sophia had immediately recognised as corresponding to different periods in history. The periods started, at the top of the object, with **Pre-history**, and ran all the way around (in the clockwise direction), through 3000 BC – 476 AD, 477 AD – 1066, 1066 – 1485, 1486 – 1601, 1602 – 1715, 1716 – 1836, 1837 – 1901, 1902 – 1945, to 1946 – 2021. After 1946 – 2021, for the last few degrees of the circle, there was an almost-blank space, marked only with the notation **'?'**.

On the mother-of-pearl face, immediately inside the Roman numerals, at the top, bottom and either side, were the letters **N, E, S** and **W**, which Sophia now knew stood for north, east, south and west, as on a compass. Then, just inside the compass letters, running clockwise in a circle from the top, were the notations 90°, 60°, 30°, 0°, 30°, 60°; and then 90°, 60°, 30°, 0°, 30° and 60° again. Sophia had learned that those notations referred to latitude and longitude – coordinates by which the location of anywhere on earth can be plotted.

Finally on the mother-of-pearl face of the PT machine, there was a faint, thin line which had been scored delicately across from IX (number 9) on the left-hand side, to III (number 3) on the right, and which therefore effectively divided the face into a top half and a bottom half. A few millimetres above the line, in the centre, was the word **Day**, and a few millimetres below the line was the word **Night**.

Several hands were also affixed to the face. All of the hands were arrow-shaped, so that they could clearly point to a number, letter, notation or word, but otherwise the hands were all different. Some were silvery, some gold, some coppery in colour. Some were shiny, some were dull. Some were plain and some were ornately carved. The various different designs made it easy to see that the different hands each related to a different set of inscriptions or notations. There were a big and a little hand that seemed to point to the time via the Roman numerals, as on a normal clock. One hand pointed steadfastly to N and another spun around to indicate direction. Together, they enabled the object to operate as a compass. A quite large hand pointed to a time period and another to Day or Night. Finally, another pair of hands (again, one big and one little) pointed to the latitude and longitude coordinates.

Sophia had soon made the marvellous deduction that the PT machine was, in fact, a time- and place-travel machine!

Sophia had realised that time and place could be altered and dictated by the moving and setting of the object's various hands. The PT machine enabled a person to go to anywhere in the world, at any point throughout history, before returning home safely, with time, in the real life present day, having stood still all the while.

Readers who have met Sophia Slewfoot before will know that Sophia had used the PT machine to take her and Toby on some amazing adventures. (Toby loved Sophia dearly and was always right by her side, taking very seriously his main task in life of protecting his darling mistress.) Sometimes the adventures took Sophia and Toby just a short distance in time and place, and sometimes they travelled across hundreds of years and thousands of miles.

However, because Sophia and Betty both lived such busy lives, ever since Sophia had discovered the PT machine there had always seemed to be something happening or someone around that prevented her from speaking secretly with her best friend. Sophia had therefore not yet managed to tell Betty all about the PT machine, never mind yet to actually use it to have an adventure together.

Today, though, that was finally about to change.

Chapter 2

Sophia Slewfoot was a very happy and outgoing girl. She was short and slight for her age, but she loved dancing, swimming and horse-riding and enjoyed playing different sports almost every day of the week. Sophia had crazy, curly blond hair which she studiously tried to tame into a plait or a ponytail every day, but which inevitably escaped its bobble after approximately five minutes. She therefore looked constantly tousled, even a bit bedraggled, no matter how hard she tried! Sophia loved her family and her devoted Beagle, Toby. Along with her best friend Betty, she had a great group of girlfriends who were always giggling and gossiping about something. When she felt unsure about something, though, or when she went somewhere new, or met someone for the first time, she could be quite quiet – sometimes even shy. She was, deep down, a thoughtful and sensitive little girl. Perhaps that was why she got on so well with Betty. Betty was tall, strong and a few months older than Sophia. She had long shining, straight blond hair and she was a confident, clever and kindly girl who was pretty-much fearless.

Together, one cautious and one carefree, they made a great team.

Today, Sophia was finally going to be able to tell Betty all about the PT machine and the incredible time-travelling adventures that she had had so far.

Sophia and Betty's school was holding a training day for the teaching staff which had been tacked on to the end of a lovely long Bank Holiday weekend. The school children had already enjoyed a weekend and an extra day off with their families. Now they very were excited to have yet another week-day day off school – a rare, and therefore very precious, occurrence. Betty's mum and dad were both working, but Sophia's mum didn't work on Tuesdays, so Betty and her younger brother Reece were coming to spend the day with Sophia and her little brother Ted. With a whole day's play date ahead of them, Sophia felt sure that today would be the day that she was finally able to go on a history's mystery-solving adventure

with her best friend. Sophia was beyond excited.

"Mum!" called Sophia the second she jumped out of bed that morning. "What time are Betty and Reece arriving?"

"Yeah Mum!" shouted Ted excitedly as he came running out of his bedroom to join Sophia. "I can't wait to play with Reece all day today – it's going to be so cool!" Ted, who was seven, had already been awake for way over an hour. He had been playing with his Lego in his bedroom for ages, as he wasn't allowed to pester their parents before seven o'clock in the morning.

"Oh, not for at least another hour yet Sophia," answered her mum, who was just getting out of bed, bleary-eyed and yearning for a good strong cup of tea. "It's still only just after 7 am. When will you two learn to start having a lie-in on weekends and holidays?!"

"Ah, ok" said Sophia. "Plenty of time, then, for me to give Betty a call to remind her what to bring. Please can I borrow your phone, Mum, please can I? I need to make sure my walkie-talkie is fully charged today, and Betty will need to do the same, so please can I borrow your phone Mum, can I please, please?!"

Sophia and Betty both had one each of a pair of walkie-talkies, which Sophia had bought with all her Christmas and birthday money added together. They were primarily for enabling Sophia and Betty to communicate when they were out and about solving mysteries, shadowing suspects and pursuing separate lines of enquiry on active investigations. However they also came in very handy for when they were not allowed to borrow and hog their parents' mobile phones. The walkie-talkies worked because the girls only lived a few streets apart in their small village.

Sophia knew, though, that of all the days since she had bought those walkie-talkies and had solemnly handed one over to Betty so as to facilitate important amateur detective business, today was the day on which it was more important than ever that the walkie-talkies were fully powered up and ready for action.

"All-right!" laughed Sophia's mum, "here you go".

"Yey! Thanks Mum" said Sophia happily as she grabbed her mum's mobile. "Oh, and if you're taking breakfast orders by any chance, while I call Bets, I'll have some cereal, toast with chocolate spread (two pieces please), some apple juice and a strawberry yoghurt. Thanks Mum, I'll be down in a min!"

Sophia's mum rolled her eyes as she made her way down the stairs, but dutifully lined up a mammoth breakfast for both of the children. They both seemed to eat pretty-much non-stop at the moment, but they were so energetic and growing so fast that they needed it, and she didn't mind at all. Besides, once she got into the kitchen, she could finally get that cuppa!

Back up in her bedroom, Sophia quickly used her mum's mobile to call Betty's parents' house phone. It was Betty who answered, quickly and excitedly (as, in fact, she did most things in life). She also used her overly posh and exaggerated telephone voice. "Hello, Babbington residence. How may I help you?!"

"Oh Bets!" laughed Sophia, "What a funny phone voice! It's only me, there's no need to sound so la-di-dah!"

"Aah, hi Sophs" replied Betty. "How come you're calling here now? I'll be over at yours shortly. What is it that can't wait 'til then?"

"It's just a really important reminder that you must bring your go-bag when you come round today."

"My go-bag?" asked Betty. "Why? I thought that we'd probably just be playing in the house and garden today. Your mum has got four kids to keep an eye on so I wasn't expecting that she'd want to go out and about anywhere, especially when two of those kids are Reece and Ted! I know we always like to be ready for anything, but I really didn't think I'd be needing my go-bag today."

For those readers that don't yet know, Sophia and Betty were both huge fans of detective books, adventure stories and whodunnit mysteries. They therefore spent a lot of their spare time learning about, and honing, their sleuthing skills. In particular, they were well aware that a good detective must always be ready for adventure and action at a moment's notice, and that they must always be prepared for anything. Sophia and Betty had therefore each assembled 'go-bags' full of essential kit, including:

- notebooks (elementary, dear reader)
- pens (several, because a detective can't afford for his or her pen to run out just when vital notes need taking)

- a torch (with spare batteries – allowing a torch to die just when you needed it most was, they knew, a real rookie error)
- binoculars
- sunglasses and a selection of hats (for when the need for a swift disguise arises)
- a paperback detective novel (for inspiration and for passing the time on stakeouts)
- a purse containing a few pounds (for emergencies)
- snacks (for energy and because, well, there's always room for snacks)
- a magnifying glass (obviously) and
- one each of the pair of walkie-talkies.

As Sophia had not yet had a chance to tell Betty about the PT machine, nor, therefore, the potential for the girls to go on time-travelling adventures without seeming to leave home even for a minute, Betty had no idea that she might need her go-bag for a simple play date at Sophia's house.

"I think you're correct that Mum isn't planning to take us and the boys out anywhere today, Bets, but I can promise you, nevertheless, that you will *definitely* need your go-bag when you come over today. It might sound crazy, but you and I will need to be ready for *anything* wherever and whenever we're going today..."

"*Wherever* and *whenever*?" interrupted Betty. "Whatever do you mean, Sophs? You're not making any sense!"

"Oh, sorry Bets" said Sophia hurriedly. "I'm afraid I haven't got time to explain just at the mo, my mum is calling me down for breakfast. Just trust me: bring your go-bag. Oh, and make sure that your walkie-talkie is fully charged!" And with that, Sophia rang off. She ran downstairs, with Toby racing along at her feet (as always), to tuck in to a hearty breakfast.

As she sat at the table with her mum and Ted, all of them enjoying the rare pleasure of a relaxed start to the day with no school, work, football, tennis or riding to rush off to, Sophia smiled secretly to herself. A big breakfast was just what she needed today. With a history's mystery adventure ahead, she was sure she was going to need lots of energy!

Chapter 3

Shortly after Sophia had finished her breakfast and had got washed and dressed for the day, the doorbell rang. Sophia's best friend, Betty Babbington, and Betty's little brother, Reece, were soon bowling into the house. They shouted "Yeah, yeah, see you!" without even a backwards glance to their dad, who was trying to explain that he would pick them up that evening after he had finished work.

Within what must have been just thirty seconds of Betty and Reece's arrival, the boys had already consumed some fruity pop and several chocolate biscuits and were deep in debate about whether to play football or Lego first. Sophia and Betty charged straight up to Sophia's bedroom. Betty was desperate to know what Sophia had meant when she had said that Betty must bring her go-bag today because it would be needed "*wherever* and *whenever*" they were going. For her part, Sophia was almost fit to burst with excitement at the prospect of finally being able to tell Betty all about the marvellous PT machine.

The second Sophia's bedroom door was closed and the girls were alone (well, except for Toby, of course), they both started speaking at once.

"You *must* tell me what's going on, Sophs!"

"Just *wait* until you hear what I've got to tell you, Bets!"

"Ok, ok!" laughed Betty, as she clambered up on to Sophia's bed and made herself comfortable amongst the cosy collection of cushions, pillows, blankets and cuddly toys. "Go on then, I'll let you explain."

Toby was torn. On the one hand, he rarely left his beloved Sophia's side, and so he had, until now, been quite happy sitting on the bedroom floor at Sophia's feet. On the other hand, however, he now saw that Betty was snuggled up and comfy-cosy on the bed. That level of snugness was pretty-much the only thing that he loved almost on a par with his darling mistress.

After hesitating for a couple of seconds, Toby reasoned that he loved Sophia's funny friend too, and the snuggly comfort of the bed was calling to him. So he leapt up and nuzzled down next to Betty, as an expectant hush fell over the room.

Sophia took a deep breath. Now that the time to share her amazing secret with Betty was here, she suddenly didn't know where to begin.

"Sophs?" prompted Betty gently.

And so Sophia began.

"Betty, do you remember when I was about to move into this house and I was really, really nervous at the end of the school day when I had to walk, for the first time, to my new 'home'?" asked Sophia. Betty nodded slowly, wondering where on earth Sophia was going with all this. "You were trying to reassure me. You were encouraging me to cheer up and you said that moving house might be the start of a great adventure."

"Ye-es" murmured Betty, calling to mind how she had wanted to stop Sophia from worrying about moving house.

"Well," said Sophia. "Betty, you were absolutely right! Moving house turned out to be the start of an incredibly exciting adventure and I cannot believe that it has taken until now before I have been able to tell you about it!"

"Go ON then!" cried Betty, who was now almost beside herself with impatience and curiosity.

"Yes of course, sorry, I'll tell you everything. So, on that very first evening, I went to explore the new house. I wasn't worried about moving anymore because, well, nothing is ever as scary as you imagine it might be, is it?! Plus, I soon realised that Tobes and I would be happy wherever we were, so long as we and our family were together. Instead, I was quite curious, and excited even, to see what secrets this 'new' (but actually very old) house might hold. Just as I was making my way along the landing upstairs to find my new bedroom, I noticed that Toby had become quite fascinated by something at the base of the wall. He had started sniffing and pawing and scratching at the skirting – something I had never seen him do before. So I decided to take a closer look."

"When I knelt down on the dusty, old carpet I saw that the skirting was not attached to the wall as I had thought. It was actually attached to an almost-concealed panel, which had no frame and was built into the wall and papered. I pushed on the panel, thinking that it must be a storage cupboard or something, but it turned out to be a secret, hidden door! Behind the door was a very tight, winding staircase that spiralled upwards towards the roof of the house. I didn't get chance to go up the stairs and investigate any further until the next day, because it was already the evening, so teatime and bedtime got in the way – it was so frustrating! The next morning, though, I climbed up the spiral staircase at the first opportunity, and I made an even more exciting discovery."

"Oooh! What was it?!" breathed Betty, who was listening quietly and intently now.

"At the top of the spiral staircase was a small, circular space. I have been calling it a hidey-hole room because it is so tiny that you can't really call it a room. It reminded me of one of those priest holes that we learned about in one of our history lessons at school. In the hidey-hole room was a safe, and inside the safe was... this!"

At this, Sophia pulled the PT machine out of her go-bag.

Betty gasped. "Wh-what's that?" she murmured, awestruck at the object's beauty and strangeness.

"This" declared Sophia "is my PT machine. It is genuinely, no kidding, honestly, truly, an actual, real life *time machine*!"

"A time machine?!" cried Betty in disbelief.

"Yes!" nodded Sophia. "A time machine, and, what's more, it's not just a machine that allows you to travel through time. It's also a machine that allows you to travel to anywhere in the world. Look, I'll show you how it works."

Sophia showed Betty the various markings on the face of the PT machine and the several different pointing hands. She explained that when a person set the hands of the PT machine to a particular historical period, a particular time of day or night, and a particular location using latitude and longitude co-ordinates, then the machine transported anyone who was in contact with it, to that exact date, time and place. To help Betty understand, Sophia pointed out that the various hands of the PT machine were currently indicating the exact time, date and location of the girls in the real life here and now: in 2021, at around 9.30 in the morning, and at the co-ordinates which Sophia knew from her research (and which she showed to Betty via the internet on her tablet) represented the specific location of their village.

"Wow" breathed Betty quietly. "That's absolutely, well, I don't know! Incredible! Is it really true?! How on earth did you discover all that, Sophs? If I had found this object I think I would probably have just taken a quick glance, thought it was just some strange sort of antique clock, and then carried on with the rest of my day without thinking any more about it."

"Well Bets," explained Sophia. "You know how much we've both enjoyed reading detective stories and learning how to be amateur sleuths? I just deployed those skills and deduced that no-one would have gone to the trouble of constructing a secret door, staircase, hidey-hole room and safe, and then hidden and locked the machine away if it wasn't some kind of big deal. I also had a bit of a breakthrough. I noticed that the whole time I was in the hidey-hole room with the PT machine, time in the real life here and now stood still. I realised that the machine therefore seemed to command time. When I found out that those notations" (Sophia indicated the latitude and longitude coordinates on the face of the PT machine) "related to location, I wondered whether it could also command place. And then... I conducted an experiment!"

"An experiment?!" asked Betty, intrigued.

"Yes!" laughed Sophia. "Actually Bets, you didn't know it at the time, but you and your family were involved in the experiment!"

With Betty looking puzzled at first and then increasingly impressed, Sophia explained how she had initially experimented with the PT machine by setting it back just a day or so from the real life present day and to the seaside village in Anglesey where (and when!), she knew, Betty was visiting her Gran. Sophia had reasoned that if anything went wrong with her first attempt at time and space travel, she could at least get home if she only travelled to a place and time from which she knew she would be able to obtain help from Betty's family if needs be.

Sophia then quickly reminded Betty about the 'history's mysteries' research project that their teacher, Mrs Taelim, had recently set for their class. Mrs Taelim had told the class that, throughout history, and despite incredible advances in science, geography and historical record-keeping over time, there have still been many incidents and happenings which remain, even to this day, unexplained. Mrs Taelim had mentioned a few examples, including the Loch Ness Monster, the Bermuda Triangle, and the princes in the Tower, but she had instructed Sophia, Betty and their classmates to use the school and village libraries and the internet to learn about some of history's unsolved mysteries.

"Bets, when I heard about that project, I used the PT machine to travel back over a hundred years and to a location in the middle of the Atlantic Ocean to investigate the mystery of a ghost ship called the Mary Celeste. I dared to do it because I had returned home safely, to the real life here and now, after the Anglesey experiment. Oh, it was soooo exciting! I actually managed to solve a mystery that had baffled people since Victorian times! I'll tell you all about my adventure with the Mary Celeste another time, Bets, but I'm getting impatient now because..."

"Because you and I are going to go on a time-travelling, history's mystery-solving adventure today, aren't we?! That's it, isn't it?! That's why you called to say that I needed to bring my go-bag?!"

Betty had leapt up off the bed, interrupted Sophia and was now running and jumping around Sophia's bedroom with her eyes shining and her face glowing with anticipation and sheer, unabashed excitement at the thought of the escapade that now lay ahead!

Chapter 4

Sophia Slewfoot had explained to her best friend Betty Babbington about her discovery of the marvellous time- and place- travelling PT machine. Never one to shy away from a challenge or the prospect of an exciting exploit, Betty had immediately agreed with Sophia that today, while Betty was at Sophia's house for a full day's play date, the girls would go on their very first time-travelling, history's mystery-solving adventure together.

"Betty, now that you know that we have the ability to visit any period throughout history and to anywhere in the world, when and where do you think we should go?" asked Sophia. She thought that, as this was Betty's first time-travelling experience, it was only fair that she should choose their destination.

"Oooh, gosh Sophs, I don't know! How did you decide to solve the mystery of the Mary Celeste when you went on your first real adventure?" asked Betty.

"I went to the library to do some research about history's mysteries, just like Mrs Taelim had suggested" said Sophia. "While I was there, Miss Reading the librarian mentioned that she had always been intrigued by that particular mystery as some of the possible theories surrounding it involved ghosts, sea monsters, magic, even pirates..."

"Pirates?!" interrupted Betty. "That gives me an idea! Pirates always make me think of buried treasure hidden away on isolated islands and, guess what?! I'm pretty sure that my mum and dad were watching something on TV the other night about a real life treasure-hunt on some far away island somewhere. Aargh, I wasn't really concentrating on what was on the telly because I was playing cards with Reece. I was only half listening to the programme in the background. Hey, though, wouldn't it be amazing if we could use the PT machine to go to that island and travel back through time to find out whether there really was some treasure buried there at some point? We could solve the mystery and, wow, just imagine, we could maybe even *find* the treasure! Oh, I really wish I could remember the name of the island or where it was."

Sophia thought that Betty's idea was great. It would be so much fun even just to go on a real life treasure-hunt, never mind also potentially solving a mystery that had baffled other treasure-hunters throughout history! Sophia was not at all put off by the fact that Betty could not remember the name or location of the island. She knew that one of the most useful things that any detective could do at the outset of a case was research.

"Just a minute, Bets" Sophia said, and she ran out of the room to grab the tablet that she shared with Ted. When Sophia returned, she suggested to Betty that they simply look up the mystery of the treasure island on the web. Sophia reasoned that even if there were lots and lots of hits on the internet about different treasure mysteries, Betty would probably recognise the name of the island that they were looking for when she saw it. Betty agreed and the girls immediately typed "island treasure mystery" into the search engine.

"That's it!" cried Betty triumphantly, as she pointed to the very first hit at the top of the search results page. "The Oak Island treasure mystery! That's exactly the mystery that I had in mind. That was definitely the island that was mentioned when my mum and dad were watching TV. I'm sure that the programme was saying that people had been searching for buried treasure on the island for hundreds of years.

Wouldn't it be soooo cool if we could solve the Oak Island mystery and find the treasure?!"

"Yes it would Bets," agreed Sophia. "Yes it would. So, let's do just that!"

Chapter 5

Sophia Slewfoot and Betty Babbington, best friends and amateur sleuths extraordinaire, had decided that they were going to use Sophia's PT machine to try to solve the mystery of the Oak Island treasure. Before they could do that, however, they needed to learn a lot more about the mystery itself. Until Sophia and Betty knew where Oak Island was, when stories about its hidden treasure began to circulate, and any other important information that they might be able to discover, the girls had no way of knowing how to begin their historical, time-travelling investigation.

"Sophs, shall we ask your mum if we can pop out to the library?" asked Betty thoughtfully. "The internet will probably be able to tell us quite a lot, but it would be great if we could also find some books about the Oak Island treasure."

"Yes, let's" said Sophia. "I'm sure my mum wouldn't mind if we went to the library for an hour or so. She's always encouraging me to use books and not always do everything on the screen. The library is so close, now that we've moved into the village centre, that you can actually see it from Ted's bedroom window!"

Sophia's assumption was correct. Her mum was happy for the two girls to visit the library. Sophia's mum had always thought that libraries were very special places. In a library anyone, from any walk of life, rich or poor, young or old, could take some precious time out of their everyday life and be transported to anywhere and any time, through reading any one of the thousands of books that lined the shelves. Even in the small local library in Sophia and Betty's village there were fiction books which told stories of adventure, romance, exploration, fantasy, comedy, tragedy, mystery, heroism, myth, legend and more. There were also non-fiction books, which explained everything that anyone could ever want to know about anything! They covered everything from the dinosaurs and Stone Age early humans of pre-history, through the history of the human race and the geography of the earth, to science, nature, religion, politics, philosophy, space and the universe!

Sophia's mum was also happy for Sophia and Betty to start to gain a little independence. The girls would, after all, be heading to high school in just over a year's time. It was therefore important that, little by little, the girls should start to build up their confidence in new places and new situations, without their parents being forever right by their side. Sophia's mum thought that a short trip to the library, which she could actually see from the house and where she knew that Miss Reading would keep a responsible eye on the girls, was a perfect opportunity for Sophia and Betty to step out on their own.

Little did Sophia's mum know that Sophia and Betty would not just be using the books in the library to transport themselves metaphorically to another place and time, oh no! They would shortly be using the PT machine to *actually* transport themselves to another place and time! The research that they would be doing in the library was merely the first step on their time-travelling, history's mystery-solving adventure!

Having got the go-ahead from Sophia's mum, Sophia and Betty grabbed their go-bags and headed over to the library. Betty was, by now, getting quite impatient to get on with the adventure, so she strode confidently up to the desk and asked Miss Reading to direct them to any books that might help them to find out more about the Oak Island treasure.

"Ooh, the Oak Island treasure?" smiled Miss Reading. "That is an exciting mystery. I can't remember all the detail, but I know that people have been hunting for treasure on Oak Island for, oh, a good couple of hundred years or so. Now, let me think. Where would we keep books that would tell you all about Oak Island? Oh yes, I think we'll have something in the history section and probably something in the geography section too..."

After just five short minutes of searching, Miss Reading had gathered together a small collection of books, all of which had some mention of Oak Island and its hidden treasure. The girls settled down with the books, and with one of the library computers so that they could do some internet research as well. These are the notes they made of what they learned:

- Oak Island (co-ordinates 44.51 °N, 64.29 °W) is one of approximately 360 small islands in Mahone Bay, Nova Scotia, Canada.

- Oak Island is tiny and, apart from treasure hunters, it is generally uninhabited.

- Rumours have been circulating since the early 1700s about wonderful, priceless treasure having been buried there.

- Rumours began with a sailor who had been aboard ship with the notorious pirate Captain Kidd (who was born around 1655 and died, executed for piracy and murder, in 1701). The sailor declared, as he was dying, that Captain Kidd had buried a hoard of treasure, worth some £2 million back in the seventeenth century (so probably worth over £2 billion — if not more, or priceless even — today), on Oak Island.

- It is widely understood that, at the end of the eighteenth century, a young man named Daniel McGinnis discovered a strange dip in the ground under an oak tree that was covered in unnatural markings. Having heard the rumours about Captain Kidd's hoard, McGinnis and his friends Anthony Vaughn and John Smith believed that they had found the site of the Oak Island treasure, and they began to dig.

● McGinnis and his friends dug down and, as they did, they discovered a shaft or pit (now known as the 'money pit'). The pit included layers of flagstones and oak platforms. It had therefore obviously been created deliberately by human hands, and was not a shaft that occurred by any natural, geographical process.

● After digging down for just over 9 metres, McGinnis and his friends stopped. Some people say that the young men were too terrified to carry on because they experienced a feeling of superstitious dread that grew stronger as they dug deeper. Other rumours suggest that the men found something in the money pit, but wanted to keep it a secret.

● Many other treasure hunting attempts since then have been unsuccessful. Often, when hunters have tried to dig deeper still, the shaft has flooded with sea water (it is on a small island in a bay of the Atlantic Ocean after all).

● So far, six hunters have died while trying to search for the Oak Island treasure. Many people believe in the 'Oak Island curse', which says that seven people must die before the treasure can be found.

● A number of items of significant historical and financial value have been discovered on Oak Island. Discoveries include a seventeenth century Spanish copper coin, an antique sword, an ancient cloth manuscript and an old parchment which many believe to be a treasure map, a medieval lead cross and a stunning blood-red rhodolite garnet gemstone. The beautiful red gem is estimated to be four hundred to five hundred years old. It is possibly part of the crown jewels of France which were lost when King Louis XVI and Marie Antoinette fled the French Revolution. (Some of those jewels have since been found, but not all...)

● Another theory is that Sir Francis Drake (Elizabethan explorer, naval commander, trader, politician and pirate) buried treasure on Oak Island. Scientists believe that Drake and his men had the engineering expertise to create the money pit and he was known to have commandeered Spanish gold, silver and jewels. Some of Drake's treasure was given to Queen Elizabeth, but much of it is likely to have been stashed away by Drake for his own private stores.

● The period 1690 to 1730 is often called the Golden Age of Piracy. Many sailors and pirates were known to travel to and around Oak Island during this time. The island enabled ships and their crews to stock up on wood, water and other important provisions. It could also be an ideal place to stash loot.

"Whoah" breathed Sophia and Betty as they both read through the assembled notes of their research.

"Pirates, gold, silver, gemstones, ancient manuscripts, lost French crown jewels, a curse causing suspicious deaths...?!" Sophia was wide-eyed at all they had learned.

"Yup" confirmed Betty, "we *definitely* need to solve the mystery of the Oak Island treasure!"

Chapter 6

Sophia and Betty had done lots of research and written-up lots of notes about the Oak Island treasure. Perhaps most importantly, they had discovered the location of the island and the most likely period in history when any treasure would have been buried. That meant that the girls could now use the PT machine to travel over the great Atlantic Ocean to Oak Island in Mahone Bay, Nova Scotia, and back in time to the Golden Age of Piracy.

The girls hurriedly packed their notes into their go-bags and called a friendly 'goodbye' to the kind librarian, Miss Reading. Sophia and Betty then raced back to Sophia's house to pack one of the most important things that any intrepid, mystery-solving explorer needs – a picnic lunch, of course!

Back at the house, Sophia realised that she would have to come up with an explanation as to why the girls needed a picnic when, as far as her mum was concerned, they would not be leaving the house. "Mum!" Sophia called. "Betty and I are playing a game where we are pretending be explorers. Please can we pack ourselves a picnic so that we can eat lunch while we are imagining that we are out and about on an adventure?"

"Yes of course" smiled Sophia's mum. "Why don't you make yourselves some ham and cheese sandwiches and grab a couple of bags of crisps and some fruit? I think there's also some of Grandma's homemade chocolate cake left, but please make sure that you leave some for Ted and Reece otherwise I'll face a riot! You know how much Ted loves Grandma's cake!"

"Thank you!" called the two girls, as they dashed to the kitchen to throw a picnic together as quickly as they could. They packed their lunch, plus a couple of extra energy bars and chocolate biscuits, along with some doggy treats for Toby. And then... it was go time!

When the girls had checked and made sure that Sophia's mum was busy downstairs and that Ted and Reece were out playing football in the garden, Sophia took Betty to the secret door that was hidden in the wall of the upstairs landing. Guided by Sophia, Betty pushed gently on the door and watched in awe as it swung open to reveal the small, spiral staircase that led up to the hidey-hole room.

In actual fact, the girls did not need to begin their adventure in the hidey-hole room. Sophia now knew that, as long as she had hold of the PT machine, then it could take her from any time and place, to any time and place. Sophia knew that Betty was keen to see the hidey-hole room and the safe, however, and she figured that setting off from there was as good a place as any to start the adventure.

The two brave and excited historical detectives, with the faithful Tobes padding along at their feet, climbed the dark and dusty staircase up into the cramped and crumbling hidey-hole room. Once there, Sophia took the PT machine out of her go-bag and turned, with a very serious expression, to face Betty.

"Betty," Sophia began. "There is just one really, really important thing that we absolutely have to remember every time that we go travelling with the PT machine, and it applies the entire time we are away too, not just when we are on the journeys to and from our destination."

"Gosh, what is it, Sophs?" asked Betty, looking somewhat alarmed. "You look so grave and serious right now that you're almost scaring me a little."

"I'm sorry," said Sophia. "I don't mean to frighten you, but there is just this one completely crucial safety briefing that I need to give you before we go any further."

As she was speaking, Sophia unbuckled the belt from her jeans and carefully looped it through the handle at the top of the PT machine. She also looped Toby's lead through her belt hooks and grabbed Betty's hand and held onto it, tight.

"Bets," explained Sophia, "I know that this is all a bit cumbersome, and I know that we've both got our walkie-talkies, but we must all absolutely remain attached to each other, and therefore to the PT machine, *at all times*. Unless we can find some rope, or some other way in which we could keep ourselves tethered together when we get to Oak Island, you must not let go of my hand *at any point, even for a second* while we are time-travelling. Whatever happens while we are on any history's mystery adventure, we and the PT machine must not, on any account, become separated. The PT machine is our only means of getting back to the real life present day, and back to the safety of our homes and families. When I conducted the Anglesey experiment, I was not holding on, or otherwise attached, to Toby and, as a result, he didn't time-travel with me. The PT machine only works when people (or dogs!) are somehow secured to it. So, if we don't hold on to the PT machine, we risk never being able to get back home, and being stuck in the mists of time. So please, whatever you do, don't let go!"

Betty, looking wide-eyed and not a little worried (which was unusual for her), nodded slowly and seriously to Sophia. "Right Sophs, understood. Don't worry, I'll hold on tight." The next minute, with a deep breath and an expression that had resumed to excitement and resolve, Betty said "So, tell me again, how does this thing work?!"

Chapter 7

Sophia reminded Betty that all they needed to do to get started on their Oak Island adventure was to set the various hands on the PT machine to the date, time and location that they wished to visit, and then hold on tight.

"I think we should probably aim to arrive on the island by no later than mid-morning," suggested Betty "as we will want plenty of time to explore before there's any chance of darkness falling."

"Yes, good thinking" agreed Sophia. "But what about the date? When, exactly, in history, do you think we should travel to?"

"Hmm," murmured Betty. "Well, one theory suggests that Sir Francis Drake left the treasure and he lived in Elizabethan times."

Sophia lifted her tablet out of her go-bag once more and began to do some further research into the famous Elizabethan explorer. She reported back to Betty. "He died at the age of around 55 or 56, something like that, in 1596. Hmm, that's quite a bit earlier than what we've learned was the Golden Age of Piracy."

"Yes," agreed Betty "and that's also quite a long time before the time of the other pirate who is rumoured to have buried treasure on Oak Island. Who was it again, oh yes, Captain Kidd." Betty consulted one of the library books in which she had read about Captain Kidd earlier that morning. "He lived from around 1655 until he was put to death for murder and piracy in 1701."

"Oh dear!" exclaimed Sophia. "It seems that the potential window of time for our investigation is actually way over a hundred years! If either of those rumours are correct, the treasure could have been buried at any time between the mid to late 1500s and the very end of the 1600s."

"It's actually even worse than that" Betty declared, looking somewhat discouraged. "The so-called Golden Age of Piracy went on until around 1730 and our research confirmed that no-one actually has any proof that treasure was buried by Drake or Kidd. In fact, treasure could have been buried by any one of, well, who knows how many pirates?"

"Oh my gosh, look at this!" Dismayed, Sophia showed Betty an internet page that she had found while Betty had been speaking. "Apparently more than 5,000 pirates were operating at sea at that time!"

"How on earth are we going to narrow down our potential window of investigation so that we can decide *when* to visit Oak Island?" groaned Betty. "The chances of us happening upon any clues as to the existence or history of the treasure if we just randomly visit at any time between the mid 1500s and 1730 are surely slim to none."

Never having been disposed to giving up in the face of adversity, however, especially when there was an adventure to be embarked upon and a history's mystery to solve, Sophia and Betty determined to take their time and think things through. One of their detective fiction heroes, Agatha Christie's Hercule Poirot, always recommended taking time out of an investigation to just *think*. He often found that by using his 'little grey cells' (his brain cells), he could uncover the solution to many a seemingly insurmountable problem. That was what Sophia and Betty determined to do now.

"I've got it!" exclaimed Sophia after just a minute or two's rumination. "We don't know when the treasure (if there is any) was buried, but we do know when rumours of its existence started circulating.

We also know when the first treasure hunters started digging. How about, as a first port of call, we visit the site and date of the McGinnis dig? There's definitely a mystery as to why McGinnis and his friends suddenly stopped digging. Perhaps if we could get to the bottom of that mystery, it would offer a clue that might help us to narrow the scope of our overall investigation?!"

"Wow, that's a great idea Sophs!" pronounced Betty. Her good humour and enthusiasm were restored immediately.

"Ok then, shall we actually do this?!" asked Sophia excitedly. "Are you holding tight? Is Toby's lead properly strapped to me? Do you want to set the PT's hands?!"

"You bet!" laughed Betty. Slowly, carefully, she turned the PT machine to face her and began to move the hands to their destination time (half past ten, **Day**), place (44.51 °N, 64.29 °W), and date (1795).

And then, with a...

Whooshkazzamflashzingwow!!! the girls and poor Tobes (who was, by now, getting used to travelling PT machine-style, although he was still not exactly keen on the experience) were off!

Sophia, Betty and Toby all felt an electrifying jolt through their bodies. They experienced a punch-like thwack in their tummy and their chest, as if all of their breath had been sucked from them for several seconds. They squeezed their eyes tight shut to protect them from the blinding glare of a flashing light that was brighter and more dazzling than anything they had ever seen before. And then, almost immediately, all was quiet and calm, and Sophia, Betty and Toby felt absolutely like themselves again.

The girls opened their eyes and were astonished, and ecstatic, to see that they were standing on a small beach in what looked like a slightly sheltered cove, with gentle waves rolling and breaking on the sandy and pebbly shore. Through hazy, pale grey morning light, the Atlantic Ocean stretched out before them as far as the eye could see, dotted here and there with tiny, tree-covered, rocky islands which were surely uninhabited. Although the weather was relatively pleasant, still and calm, the ocean outside the cove was violently roiling and churning, whipping white-capped surf against the rocky outcrops of the surrounding islands and battering them with a frenzied and frightening force. It was therefore immediately evident to Sophia and Betty why Oak Island, on which they had clearly landed, had been a sanctuary destination for pirates and sailors throughout maritime history.

Oak Island

Behind Sophia, Betty and Tobes, densely wooded land rose towards the centre of the island. Through the bushy scrubland where the beach merged into the forest, the girls could just make out a rough path. Consulting the compass hands on the PT machine, the girls reasoned that, in one direction, the path lead around the cove towards the west and, in the other, it lead into the woodland and climbed upwards and northwards. It was from the northerly direction that a loud, methodical, tapping sound suddenly disturbed the otherwise almost-complete silence which surrounded them.

"What's that noise d'you think Sophs?" asked Betty. She had a smile and glint in her eye which showed that she was sure that following the sound would be the girls' first step towards solving the Oak Island treasure mystery.

"I've no idea Bets" grinned Sophia in reply, "but I'm guessing we're agreed that we're going to investigate?!"

"Absolutely!" cried Betty. And so the funny little party – two ten year old girls, one tall and strong and one small and slight with a strange antique clock-like device banging at her hip, both tethered to the lead of their faithful and friendly Beagle – clambered off, somewhat clumsily, to climb the roughly hewn path as it disappeared into the trees.

Chapter 8

Having used the marvellous PT machine to travel to Oak Island, Nova Scotia, in the year 1795, Sophia, Betty and Toby were making their way, quietly and carefully, along an uneven track through dark and otherwise impenetrable woodland. They could hear a regular knock-knock-knocking sound that seemed too loud to come from a woodpecker or other bird or creature. Neither girl had voiced their wishes to the other for fear of jinxing their early good luck, but both Sophia and Betty were hoping that the noise was coming from the McGinnis treasure hunting party.

The girls had done some quite detailed research before setting off on such a daring adventure. As a result, they both knew (and the PT machine's compass confirmed) that they were walking, stealthily and steadily, in a north-easterly direction from the cove on which they had landed. The cove had been at the south side of the small island. The girls were therefore both quietly confident that, if their suppositions and calculations were correct, they were moving directly towards the location of the famous Oak Island 'money pit'.

After around an hour's trek, throughout which Toby had been happily padding and snuffling along just the little way ahead of the girls that his lead allowed, Toby suddenly came to an abrupt halt. He pricked up his ears and raised his head to sniff the air. Sophia and Betty noticed that, all of a sudden, his hackles were up. That is, the hairs running all along his spine were standing on end, as they did when Toby was at his most alert and most ready to protect his beloved girls.

Sophia and Betty slowed to a stop as well. Instinctively, without saying a word to Toby or to each other, the girls crept off the track and crouched down into the cover of the bushy undergrowth. It was a good job they had done so because, just a few seconds later, a youngish man, whose clothes were tattered, wet and absolutely covered in mud, came rushing along the rough path with a horrified look on his face. The man was carrying a huge sack which he had slung over his shoulder and which was bulging and weighed down with what appeared to be bulky, clinking contents.

"Hey, come back Johnny!" called another man's voice, from a short distance away in the direction from which the scruffy man was hurrying. The man's voice had a slight drawl to it, a bit like the accents which Sophia and Betty recognised from the American TV shows they watched at home, but not quite. ('Canadian' thought Sophia to herself.) "Come on, I know you're scared and I don't blame ya, but surely there's more for us to find here. It's gotta be worth the risk, man. Come on, come back, we need your help, bud!"

"No way, Dan, I ain't doing this no more!" shouted back the young man. "I'm not coming back and I'm not doing no more digging. It's not worth it! We need to quit while we're ahead, man. We need to quit while we've still got our lives!" And then, without another word or another look back, the man ran off through the forest, heading in the direction from which Sophia, Betty and Toby had just come, his heavy sack bouncing and clunking as he went.

Sophia and Betty, still hidden and silent in the scrubby bushes on the forest floor, glanced at each other with a knowing smile. 'Dan' must be Daniel McGinnis and 'Johnny' must be his friend and fellow treasure hunter John Smith! The girls knew that they really were on the right track!

Bolstered by the realisation that they could be within spitting (or hearing!) distance of finding out why the McGinnis party stopped digging for the Oak Island treasure, Sophia and Betty inched their way on their hands and knees towards the direction of Daniel's voice. In just a few steps (well, crawls) the girls noticed that the undergrowth was thinning. The forest was giving way to an earth-covered clearing on what appeared to be the summit of the higher ground that they had been able to see when they had glanced upwards from the sandy cove below.

In the centre of the clearing was a large, circular shaft that had been dug into the ground and shored up all around with wooden planks. Scattered around the rim of the shaft were a collection of discarded spades, shovels, buckets, knives, ropes, wheelbarrows, logs and all sorts of other paraphernalia clearly associated with a digging expedition. Another young man, tallish, sturdily-built and handsome but also completely filthy and with tatty, torn shirtsleeves and ragged trousers, was standing at the rim of the shaft. He was pulling with all his might on a rope, one end of which was tied around his waist while the other disappeared down the hole.

"Betty," whispered Sophia in awe. "This is it! We've found the money pit!"

Chapter 9

As Sophia, Betty and Toby watched from their hidden lookout on the edge of the clearing in which the Oak Island money pit was located, the young man at the rim of the pit, whom Sophia and Betty believed must be Daniel McGinnnis, began backing slowly away from the edge. As he walked slowly and steadily backwards, he was heaving up, out of the money pit, the rope which was tied around his waist and onto which he was clinging as if for dear life. It soon became clear why. After a few more strained steps, the arms and then the head and chest of a third man appeared out of the top of the money pit. The third man slumped half in, half out of the shaft as the tall man collapsed in a heap on the ground, obviously exhausted from the effort of hauling his friend out of the pit.

The third man, hunched over with the top half of his body sprawled over the rim of the shaft and his legs still hanging down inside the money pit, was drenched. Wet hair covered his face and his soaking clothes clung to his skin. From where Sophia and Betty were secretly surveying the situation, it was obvious that the man was shivering. As the day was actually fairly warm, Sophia and Betty wondered whether the man was feeling cold because he was sopping wet, or whether in fact he was shaking from shock, or even fear. Before the girls had time to give that question any real thought, however, and before they had time to discuss what they were seeing or to plan the next steps in their investigation, disaster struck!

As the third man roused himself and tried to pull himself fully out of the money pit, the knot which had secured the other end of the rope around Daniel's waist began to unravel. Daniel was still lying down, worn out, on the ground and so he didn't realise immediately the danger that his friend was now in – the danger of falling back down, entirely unsecured this time, into the obviously deep, wet, perilous pit.

Sophia, Betty and even Tobes, however, *did* realise. In a flash, without any thought in their heads except trying to save another person from harm, all three leapt out from their hiding place and flung their full weight down on to the ground on top of the rope, which was now speedily skidding and sliding downwards, towards and into the gaping shaft. As they fell on to the rope, Sophia and Betty grabbed at it and clung on with every ounce of strength in their bodies, desperately hoping to save the falling man from disappearing down the shaft altogether.

The combined weight and strength of two ten year old girls and a Beagle was, unfortunately, not enough to counter gravity and the weight of a falling full grown man.

It *was* enough, though, to slow down the man's plummet just enough to give Daniel McGinnis time to jump up and leap into action once again, to grab the tumbling rope and to add his full weight and strength to the effort to save his friend.

To everyone's immense relief, the teamwork worked! Sophia, Betty, Toby and Daniel McGinnis felt an abrupt, sharp jerk as the third man (who must, Sophia realised, be Anthony Vaughn) stopped

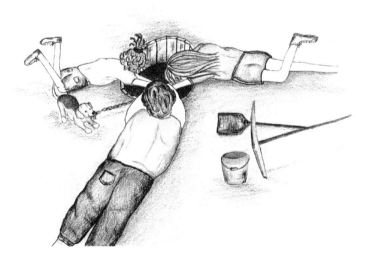

falling at last. The girls, Toby and Daniel all then began the laborious process of hauling the man out of the money pit once more, only this time Daniel did not rest when Antony's soaking head and shoulders appeared at the rim. Instead, this time, Daniel immediately ran to the edge of the money pit, placed his hands under Anthony's arms, and dragged the shocked and soaking man out of the shaft and, finally, to safety.

It was only at this point that the men whom Sophia and Betty had guessed to be treasure hunters Daniel McGinnis and Anthony Vaughn turned to look at, and to actually take in the extraordinary sight of, the strange little party that had come to their rescue.

And to the men the party seemed very strange indeed!

Quite apart from the fact that Sophia was tied to her dog and had a clock-like machine strapped to her belt, the men noticed that, despite the fearless, frantic, life-saving dive that they had just undertaken, the two girls' hands remained clasped together at all times, as if they were terrified to let go. That seemed at odds with the bravery that the girls had just demonstrated when leaping to the aid of the falling man. On top of all of that, Daniel and Anthony couldn't seem to fathom the completely unexpected, completely *inexplicable*, sight of two young girls, clearly healthy, relatively wealthy and wholly out of place on this harsh, largely uninhabited island. Furthermore, the girls were wearing clothes the like of which the men had simply never seen: one of them in denim cut-off shorts and the other wearing sporty clothes made out of some sort of stretchy, shiny material which he had *never* encountered before[2]. Who were these girls, and from where (and when?!) had they come?!

At the same time, it suddenly dawned on both Sophia and Betty that, having revealed themselves to Daniel and Anthony in the heat of the emergency rescue, they had exposed themselves, without thinking, to the hazards of the time-traveller's paradox. That is, that any action taken by a time-traveller in the past

---

2   *For any readers who may be history enthusiasts like Sophia herself, denim jeans were not invented until 1871 – nearly eighty years after Sophia and Betty visited Oak Island in 1795. Even then they were generally only worn by workmen and cowboys. Jeans were not widely worn by women and girls until the 1970s onwards – some 175 years after Sophia and Betty's encounter with the McGinnis treasure hunting party! Spandex (or elastane/Lycra), the stretchy, sporty material that is now so common in a huge range of comfortable, casual clothes for men, women and children, was not invented until 1958. It was used only in underwear until as late as the 1990s!*

could cause untold ripple effects which could affect the future, and which could even affect the real here and now of Sophia and Betty's home life in the present day. The 1985 film 'Back to the Future'[3] had probably demonstrated the problem most effectively. It explained that the ripple effects could be dangerous, potentially even resulting in the purpose for time-travelling, or even the time-traveller him- or herself, ceasing to exist!

For a few moments, Sophia, Betty, Toby, Daniel and Anthony all stood still, silently staring at each other and wondering what on earth to think or say.

But then, all of a sudden, Anthony burst into a great big grin and said, with a strong Canadian drawl and with friendly laughter in his eyes, "Well, what in the world do we have here then?! Are you girls some funny-looking angels that have fallen down from heaven just to save little ol' me from a-falling down to my death in this-here hell-hole pit?!"

At the thought of being called angels Sophia and Betty couldn't help but giggle! With a quick

---

3   *A Steven Spielberg film. Written by Robert Zemeckis and Bob Gale, directed by Zemeckis.*

affirmative glance between themselves and with a nod to the fact that Tobes' hackles had gone down and he had begun to playfully sniff and nuzzle the men (thereby confirming that they were no threat), the girls decided to come clean and to explain their mystery-solving mission. After all, they reasoned, a first-hand interview of key contemporary witnesses could prove an invaluable opportunity to gather crucial evidence to help the girls on their way!

Chapter 10

Having accidentally revealed their presence on Oak Island to treasure hunters Daniel McGinnis and Anthony Vaughn, Sophia and Betty (still holding tight to each other and tethered to Toby and the PT machine) showed the young men that the PT machine was, in fact, a time- and place- travel machine. The girls explained that the machine allowed Sophia and Betty to investigate real life mysteries from throughout history. They also explained how essential it was that the girls did not impinge too much upon events in their past (that is, during whatever time in history they were visiting), in case the consequences of their interference ended up being harmful for the girls, for anyone they came into contact with, or for the overall course of history, in some as yet unknown way.

Bit by bit the men's disbelief dissipated, and gave way to awe, admiration and delight. They were impressed with the amazing PT machine, and with the brave and exuberant Sophia and Betty. As soon as they had come to terms with the fact that they were speaking with two children from the future, Daniel and Anthony confirmed that they had indeed been digging for the Oak Island treasure. They started to explain what they had found, and why their friend and fellow-digger John Smith had just abandoned the escapade in fright.

"It all began" said Daniel "when I noticed that the ground right in the centre of this-here clearing was different – it was sunken somewhat. Next I noticed that that tree over yonder was covered in strange, surely unnatural markings. I thought to myself that markings on a tree might just be a good way of noting the spot where a person had buried treasure. Then, a couple days later, I figured that ground which had been disturbed by burying treasure might just be dipped and soft and sunk a little as a result. I got myself to thinkin' about the old Captain Kidd rumours and I said to myself 'that's it Dan, you're a-goin' treasure huntin'!' I couldn't get the idea outta my head that there was somethin' down there, somethin' really, really worth findin'. In just another few days, me and my buddies were diggin' and, y'know what? I was right! That really is a true, real life, treasure trove! It really is, man!"

"Yes," cut in Anthony "and we really did start to

make some real amazin' discoveries. Almost right away we saw that the shaft was deep, real deep, man, and that it was shored up all around with these huge wooden planks. We thought about everyone that we knew all around this here Mahone Bay and we knew that no-one had the tools or the skill to dig and bolster a shaft like that. We knew that this must have been created by someone special, perhaps with a whole fleet of helpers..."

"And then we found all sorts of old, old bits and bobs. Sea-farin' stuff y'know. We found a top class, expensive-looking sextant that was engraved with the date 1581 and the words 'Under Royal Warrant to Her Majesty the Queen' or somethin' like that, so we figured that at least some of this stuff must have originated from England, way, way over the ocean, man. We found pots and pans and what looked like a ship's log[4], but the ink had faded so much that we could hardly make out the name of the vessel.

---

[4] *A ship's log is an important record of the management, operation and navigation of a ship. If and when anything goes wrong with a ship (bad weather, loss of life, loss of cargo, acts of piracy, and the like), the log is a crucial means of establishing what happened.*

It included the word 'Rosa' or 'Rosary' or somethin' like that. Then things started to go wrong. It seemed like every time we found something treasure-like – solid silver cutlery and candlesticks, that kinda thing – somethin' real bad happened. A part of the shaft collapsed; one of us had a fall; the sky clouded right over and the world went real dark and real quiet on an otherwise sunny day; stuff like that," said Daniel.

"Yeah, it got kinda scary," agreed Anthony. "We started to get a real bad feelin' and we started to have more and more accidents when we were diggin'. One day we found a few gold coins (they've got foreign writing on them which might be Spanish or Portuguese or somethin', probably from the times of some of them famous European explorers) and Johnny immediately had a really bad fright. The rope that had been tied around his middle while he was a-diggin' down in the pit, a really thick, strong, sturdy rope (or so we thought), suddenly just snapped right in two and he went plungin' right down into the depths, man. And you know there's water down there, don't ya? He nearly drowned. It was only the fact that Daniel happened to be in the pit at the same time and had a spare rope over his shoulder that saved ol'

Johnny's life."

"That spooked Johnny real, real bad" explained Daniel. "Even Tony and me started to feel like there was somethin' wrong, somethin' bad. Some strange, evil force at work in this 'ere shaft. There have been murmurings for years about pirates burying treasure and then cursing the land so that any fella who comes a-huntin' comes a-cropper, but we had never given those murmurs much mind until recently. Johnny was a bit more superstitious than us two, though, so he has been having doubts for a good few days now. I think that when Tony's rope failed just now and he also went a crashin' down into the deep, dark, depths, that was somethin' of a last straw for ol' Johnny boy."

Sophia and Betty looked at each other thoughtfully. They both remembered reading about the fact that the McGinnis party had been overcome with dread the more they dug in the pit. They also remembered the history books talking about an Oak Island curse that had, by the year 2021, claimed the lives of six treasure hunters, none of whom were from the McGinnis party. While on the one hand Sophia and Betty were reluctant to interfere with historical events, on the other hand they did want to do whatever they could to help and protect these friendly young men. Perhaps if they told the men about the curse then they would simply be ensuring that history remained that way? That is, that none of the McGinnis party would perish in the pit?

After a quick chat between themselves, Sophia and Betty decided to share their knowledge from the 'future' (that is, from Sophia and Betty's real life present day) with Daniel and Anthony, and to beg them not to continue with their dig.

For their part, Daniel and Anthony were so impressed by these brave and clever little girls, that they absolutely took on board all that the girls were trying to explain. They agreed at once not to dig for treasure on Oak Island any more, realising that health and happiness (which Sophia and Betty both possessed in abundance!) were much more important in life than riches and physical possessions. Daniel and Anthony also recognised that finding the treasure had already started to disrupt their lives. It had endangered them all and it had caused arguments and a rift between them and their old friend John Smith. In addition, the stress of not knowing what the treasure was, who it had belonged to, whether keeping it meant that they were stealing, or even what they should do with it if they *did* keep it, had already been causing them anxiety for some time.

So, with their hearts and minds feeling lighter and more carefree than they had done for days, the young men thanked Sophia and Betty for their visit and for their wise words from the 'future'.

"I'm just sorry that we haven't been able to shed any light on the mystery of the treasure for you though, Miss Sophia and Miss Betty" mourned Anthony. I wish that there was something that we could do to really help."

"There is perhaps one thing that you could do to help" exclaimed Betty all of a sudden, a brilliant brain-wave having just that second swept over her.

"What's that then?!" asked the men and Sophia, all at once.

"Please can you let us see the ship's log and one of the foreign coins that you found? They could turn out to be really valuable clues as to who buried the treasure or where it came from. When we go back to the future, to our own real life present day, that is, we can hit the books again. (Betty didn't bother

71

mentioning the internet – how on earth would she explain *that* to Daniel and Anthony in eighteenth century Mahone Bay?!) We can probably use any information that we can glean from the log book and the coin to more accurately focus our investigation. That could really help us to decide where and when to go for the next stage of our history's mystery-solving expedition!"

"Wow, that's a brilliant idea, Bets!" laughed Sophia, and the kind young men agreed.

"We can do even better than that" smiled Daniel. "We can give them to you to keep! Here you go." With that, he pulled out of his breast pocket a dirty, tattered and crumpled leather-bound book, along with a muddy, but otherwise shining, golden coin. "Take them, please. We don't need them. We can't do anything with them, but you might be able to. Just think, in the year 2021 (2021 Tony, what about that?!), you might be able to actually solve the mystery that we started to unearth right here in 1795. That would really make us a part of somethin' kinda special, I reckon!"

"Oh wow, thank you so much" said Sophia and Betty in unison. Tobes also snuggled appreciatively against Daniel's legs. The girls gratefully, and very carefully, took the old ship's log and the grubby, but otherwise untarnished, coin. Betty placed them delicately in her go-bag, wrapped up in a hoody to keep them as protected as possible until the girls could get the precious artefacts home and safe.

"And here, take this from us too" said Anthony as he untied from his waist and handed over to Sophia a long, thin but incredibly tightly woven, and therefore very strong, rope. "This is our best, tried and tested, safety rope. I reckon you two'll be able to move around much more freely and get up to much more derring dos on your time-travellin' adventures if you are tied together by a length of rope, instead of having to hold hands at all times. After all, you've saved my life today and I ain't goin' to be needin' this 'ere lifeline no more now."

Sophia and Betty were truly touched. They understood that the safety rope was a really thoughtful gift that would definitely come in very handy on future escapades. It would, from this point on, be a new staple in Sophia's go-bag and it would always remind the girls of their late eighteenth century eventful encounter with the McGinnis Oak

Island treasure hunters. For the time being, though, the rope provided a great opportunity for Sophia and Betty to tether themselves safely together, and also allowed them to each have the use of both their hands as they readied themselves for the journey back to their home village in 2021.

Daniel and Anthony watched in amazement and waved excitedly to the girls as Sophia moved the hands of the PT machine back to the latitude and longitude coordinates that would take her, Betty and Toby back home. Before they knew it, with a whooshkazzamflashzingwow!!!, the plucky girls and their friendly little dog had disappeared right before Daniel's and Anthony's very eyes.

And in a matter of seconds – literally in a flash! – Sophia, Betty and Toby found themselves back in the hidden hidey-hole room.

Betty, who was both flabbergasted by her first ever time-travelling adventure and buzzing with excitement and relief at having arrived safely back at Sophia's house, burst out into a great big grin. "Wow Sophs!" she cried. "That was fantastic! Incredible! Absolutely, completely, fabby, fabby doo!"

"I'm so glad you could come with me today, Bets" laughed Sophia. "And I'm so pleased that we met Daniel McGinnis and Anthony Vaughn. Not only have we potentially saved them from falling victim to the Oak Island curse, but also we've picked up what I'm sure will be some vital clues to help us with our history's mystery-solving quest.

"I know!" nodded Betty. "You know what, though? I've just realised that we've been away for *hours*, but listen – that's your mum calling Ted and Reece in for lunch. It really is as if no time at all has passed in the here and now! That's great and everything, but it does mean that we've been on the go for *ages* and we've been so busy that we forgot to eat our picnic. I'm *starving* now!"

"Ha ha, me too!" giggled Sophia. "Come on then, let's leave our analysis of the evidence until later. The log book and the coin are still in your go-bag aren't they? We can store them securely in the safe for now and we can take our lunch downstairs and eat it with the boys and my mum. It will seem just as if we've never been away anywhere or *anywhen* at all. They'll never suspect a thing!"

With that, the two hungry but happy girls stored

the invaluable artefacts in the safe and ran merrily down to Sophia's kitchen for a very overdue 'picnic' lunch.

Chapter 11

After a satisfying lunch of sandwiches, crisps, fruit, biscuits, slices of Grandma's delicious chocolate cake and some fizzy pop, the girls told Sophia's mum that they wanted to head back upstairs to continue with their imaginary explorer game.

"Ah no, girls" said Sophia's mum. "You've been inside pretty much all morning and the sun is coming out now. Can't you play your game in the garden and get some fresh air at the same time? Poor Toby is happy to stick by your side as always, but I'm sure he'd love the chance to have a bit of a run around outside. You could perhaps even take him for a nice walk a bit later. That would really help me out, actually, as the boys will definitely moan if I try and drag them out on a dog walk with Toby and me."

"Ok Mum, that's no problem" nodded Sophia. With a knowing wink to Betty, she added "we can play our game from anywhere! We just need to grab a few things from upstairs, then we'll go and do our 'exploring' in the garden."

Since Sophia's family had moved into their new (but nearly 300 year old) home, her mum and dad had been slowly but surely trying to renovate the somewhat tumbledown house and its rambling, overgrown garden. Although they had so far made some progress, the garden still remained somewhat wild and unkempt, and it felt to the children like a wonderful wilderness, full of places to play and hide. Over the recent Bank Holiday weekend, Sophia and Ted had used sticks and small branches, which had fallen from the tall trees which loomed over the bottom of the garden, to construct a den under cover of the trees' lush, dense, low hanging leaves. Sophia and Betty carried a cosy blanket, their go-bags, their water bottles, a few extra snacks (well, there's always room for extra snacks), the library books that they had borrowed earlier that morning, and Sophia's tablet all down to the relative privacy of the den.

It was time for the intrepid amateur detectives to devise the next phase of their history's mystery-solving mission!

After spreading out their blanket and making themselves as comfortable as possible, Sophia and Betty (with Tobes curled up contentedly between them) turned their attention to the two fascinating artefacts that Daniel McGinnis and Anthony Vaughn had recovered from the Oak Island money pit in 1795. Betty ever-so gently lifted out of her go-bag the hoody in which the items were wrapped. She softly and slowly peeled back the layers of padded, fleecy material to reveal an old, battered, worn and faded ship's log book and a dirt-covered, but otherwise untarnished, gold coin.

"Wow" breathed Sophia quietly. "I can hardly believe my eyes. We are sitting here in my back garden in 2021, but we are in possession of historical records and treasure that pre-date 1795, possibly by hundreds of years. This book and coin were most likely buried by real life, actual pirates and they could be the clues which set us on the road to actually solving the mystery of the Oak Island treasure."

"I know" said Betty, reverently. She could feel a tingle running up and down her spine as she thought about how very special these artefacts were. She also felt a thrill of anticipation at the prospect of yet more time-travelling adventures still to come. "Let's examine the evidence then, shall we?"

With that, the girls turned, first, to the ship's log. The parchment that made up the pages of the book was, unfortunately, so badly ravaged from being buried in amongst wet mud and sand for who knows how many years that it had almost turned to dust. It crumbled in the girls' hands as soon as they tried to touch it or turn any of the pages. What's more, the damp and dirt from the depths of the money pit had, over time, faded and washed out the text that had been written on the parchment. It had become, certainly to the girls' naked eyes, without the benefit of the specialist scientific tools and techniques that would be available to expert archaeologists and museum conservators, completely illegible.

To make things even worse, any scraps of writing that could still be made out at all, seemed to be in a foreign language. Sophia and Betty had learned a little bit of French for fun at a lunchtime school club a couple of years ago, and they knew that they would have the opportunity to learn more French, as well as Spanish or German when they went to High School. For the time being, however, trying to make out any of the largely deteriorated foreign script from the pages of the log, was simply beyond our heroic historical sleuths.

"Oh dear, it's such a shame that we can't learn anything from the crumbling contents of the log itself," stated Sophia "but it's definitely not the end of the road for our analysis of this book."

"Isn't it?" asked Betty, looking puzzled. She had started to worry that they wouldn't be able to learn anything of any use from the old log book after all, and she was in danger of becoming a little disheartened.

"No, not at all" explained Sophia. "Perhaps the most valuable thing would be if we could discover the name of the ship from which this log came. I'm sure that if we had the ship's name we could quite easily do some research to find out when it had sailed, who had captained it, and whether there are any other historical facts that could shed light on the mystery."

"You're absolutely right, Sophs!" cried Betty. "Good thinking! Oh, and didn't Daniel or Anthony mention something about the log showing the name of the vessel somewhere – I think they said it was 'Rosa' or 'Rosary' or something like that?"

"Yes," agreed Sophia "and look! This must have been where they got that information."

Slowly, delicately and with the utmost care, Sophia used the edge of their clean, soft, woollen blanket to brush away some of the mud and sand that had clung to the worn and torn leather of the log book's front cover. Bit by bit Sophia was able to reveal the following scrap of sprawling, old-fashioned script:

estra Señora del Rosari

"estra Señora del Rosari?" queried Betty, thoughtfully. "What on earth does that mean? And have you noticed that it doesn't start with a capital letter? I thought that names were always given capital letters. Is that not the case in other languages? Is this not a vessel's name after all, or are some letters or words perhaps missing? I don't really know what to make of this Sophs, do you?"

"I think that you might be on to something with the idea that maybe some letters or words are missing, Bets" mused Sophia. "The old leather cover is full of holes and there are tears around much of its raggedy edge. I think that this book has been beaten and battered about for many, many years while it has been buried in the money pit. Perhaps it has even been sloshed around in the sea water that we know rises up into the pit from time to time. As a result, I think it is quite possible that some lettering or wording has simply worn away. I'm hoping that we've got enough to go on, though. Don't you remember that lots of detectives and police men and women in the various mystery stories that we have read can often trace a person or a car via a 'partial' fingerprint or a 'partial' registration plate? Well, perhaps we can trace the name of the ship with this 'partial' title?"

"I hope you're right Sophs!" smiled Betty enthusiastically. "If so, we might really be starting to get somewhere with this history's mystery!" As she spoke, Betty was tapping the phrase 'estra Señora del Rosari' into the search engine on Sophia's tablet.

Internet coverage within the tree-covered den at the bottom of Sophia's garden was intermittent at best and it seemed to the two historical detectives that the search results were taking an *age* to load. However patience is, of course, a virtue, and the girls' waiting was soon rewarded with a clear hit.

"Spanish ship Nuestra Señora del Rosario, 1587!" read Betty triumphantly.

The girls then quickly skim-read the available information from this spot-on search result, and jotted down the following key points in one of the notebooks from Sophia's go-bag:

- The Nuestra Señora del Rosario was one of the first-rate ships in the Armada of the Kingdom of Spain in service between 1587 and 1588.

- The Rosario was part of the fleet of Spanish ships that attempted to invade England in 1588.

- As it swept up the English Chanel under cover of darkness one night in July of that year, Sir Francis Drake, in charge of the defending English fleet, pursued and captured the Rosario.

"Sir Francis Drake!" exclaimed Sophia. "I'm sure he cropped up in the research that we undertook in the library this morning."

"Gosh, was that really just this morning?!" laughed Betty. "So much has happened since then that it seems like days and days ago, doesn't it?!"

But Sophia wasn't listening. "Yes, here it is," confirmed Sophia, showing their notes from earlier in the day to Betty, and going on to read:

A theory is that Sir Francis Drake (Elizabethan explorer, naval commander, trader, politician and pirate) buried treasure on Oak Island. Scientists believe that Drake and his men had the engineering expertise to create the money pit and he was known to have commandeered Spanish gold, silver and jewels. Some of Drake's treasure was given to Queen Elizabeth, but much of it is likely to have been stashed by Drake for his own private stores.

"Wowweee, that's it!" whooped Betty. "We've done it! We've solved the mystery of the Oak Island treasure!"

"Well, I agree that we've certainly made a good start, Bets" nodded Sophia slowly, "but I've got a nagging feeling that we don't yet know the whole story..."

Chapter 12

While Betty was generally the more confident, outgoing and forthright of our terrific, time-travelling twosome, the virtues of patience, diligence and attention to detail were sometimes more Sophia's strong suit. If it had been entirely up to Betty, she would, with their discovery of Sir Francis Drake's definite connection to the Oak Island money pit, have been ready to announce to the world that they had solved the mystery. Sophia was a serious and studious history buff, though. She understood the importance of conscientiously and meticulously checking and cross-referencing facts and findings to build up a complete and accurate picture of past events. It was to that painstaking process that Sophia turned now, as she reviewed, once again, the notes that they had made earlier in the day.

After several moments of quiet and careful reading, Sophia suddenly shouted "That's it! That's what has been nagging at me. I think that the log book from the Nuestra Señora del Rosario does prove that Sir Francis Drake buried treasure on Oak Island (especially when you take into account the fact that the pit was clearly constructed by a fleet of talented engineers, and probably ship's joiners, who had access to the best tools, just like Drake's copious crew would have done). But that isn't enough to explain the whole of the mystery. I thought that we had come across a clue somewhere that suggested that there must be other treasure buried there too, and I was right. Look!"

With that, Sophia pointed out to Betty an extract from the notes from their earlier research:

A number of items of significant historical and financial value have been discovered in the money pit... Discoveries include a seventeenth century Spanish copper coin...

"Ye-es," said Betty a little unsurely. "I know that other items have been discovered, but I don't understand why that is an issue for us."

"The issue is that one of the other items discovered was from the *seventeenth* century and..."

"Ah, I see!" interrupted Betty, privately marvelling at how clever and perceptive Sophia had been.

"Sir Francis Drake was around in the 1500s, but a seventeenth century Spanish coin was also discovered. The seventeenth century was the 1600s. There's no way that Sir Francis Drake can have buried a coin that hadn't even been created yet during his lifetime!"

"Exactly, Bets, exactly" said Sophia. "Sir Francis Drake cannot have buried a seventeenth century coin, so that means..."

"That means that someone *else also* buried treasure in the Oak Island money pit!" shouted Betty as she interrupted once again, this time out of sheer exhilaration caused by the historical deduction process. "Someone who came along several years, perhaps even a hundred years or more, *after* Sir Francis Drake!"

"Yes" stated Sophia. "So that means, to paraphrase the great literary detective Sherlock Holmes, the game is still afoot![5]"

---

5   Interestingly, although today it is Sir Arthur Conan Doyle's detective extraordinaire, Sherlock Holmes, who is most commonly associated with the phrase 'the game is afoot', in fact the phrase is actually understood to have originated with William Shakespeare, who used it in at least two of his plays: Henry IV Part I and Henry V.

Betty was beaming as Sophia spoke. She was having so much fun on her first ever history's mystery-solving mission. On the one hand she would have been over the moon if the girls had managed to solve the mystery of the Oak Island treasure so quickly and easily, but on the other she would perhaps have been a bit disappointed if their treasure-hunting journey had not involved another time-travelling trip. With the recognition that Sir Francis Drake's involvement was only one piece of the puzzle, Betty realised that there would indeed be more adventures to come!

"Let's get back to our analysis of the evidence then, Sophs!" suggested Betty eagerly. "Perhaps if we examine the coin that Daniel and Anthony found, it will give us another clue and indicate another avenue of enquiry for us to follow on our quest!"

Chapter 13

Amateur historical sleuths Sophia Slewfoot and Betty Babbington (along with their faithful sidekick Toby the Beagle) were huddled together in a twig- and branch-built den at the bottom of Sophia's wild and overgrown garden. They were deeply engrossed in formulating the next phase of their pursuit to uncover the truth of the enduring Oak Island treasure mystery.

The girls had, through a clever combination of research, analysis, oh, and time-travel via the amazing PT machine of course, established that the Oak Island money pit had more than likely been constructed by the English Elizabethan explorer (and, according to certain sources, state-endorsed pirate) Sir Francis Drake. They had also realised, however, that Drake could not have been the only person to hide treasure on Oak Island, as some of the treasure that had been discovered post-dated Drake's death. The girls were therefore now turning their attention to the grubby, mud-covered coin that the eighteenth century McGinnis treasure hunters had given to them.

"I think that the first thing we need to do with this coin, Sophs, is to clean it up. We can then hopefully see some of the detail on its two faces. We might be able to reveal a date or some text or other engravings which could shed some light on its origins. If we can discover where and when the coin came from, we might be able to work out how it came to be buried on Oak Island."

"I agree" said Sophia, "but we will need something very gentle with which to clean the coin. We are assuming it is gold because, underneath the mud, it looks as if the coin has not deteriorated at all over time. If it's not actually gold, though, if it is some other metal, there's a chance that certain cleaning fluids or chemicals could damage it."

"Yes, but I don't think that we can take the coin up to the house to wash it with water in the sink," mused Betty "because your mum might see us doing that, and she could ask some quite awkward questions about where we got it!"

"Hmm, you're right" nodded Sophia thoughtfully. "Hey, I know! What about using baby wipes?! I'm sure they say on the packet that they are mild enough to use on newborn babies' skin, so they can't have any harsh chemicals in them, surely. Also, my mum has packets and packets of them to hand in pretty-much every room of the house. She's constantly chasing Ted round with them making sure he doesn't wipe his sticky fingers on his clothes, the furniture, or the windows!"

"Ha ha! Good thinking Sophs! Why don't you run and get a pack of wipes, then, while I use the edge of this blanket to start getting off the worst of the mud?"

With that, Sophia shot up to the house to grab some wipes. While she was there, she had another bright idea. She quickly gathered together a pad of paper and a soft, velvety drawing pencil, which she also took back down to Betty.

"Bets, have you ever done coin-rubbing?" asked Sophia.

"Erm, no, I don't think I have" answered Betty. "What's that?"

"It's a really effective technique for discovering what markings are engraved onto coins or other pieces of metal" explained Sophia. "When the coin or metal is as clean as you can get it, you place a thin sheet of paper over it (ideally working on a table or other flat surface – we could use the thick cardboard back of this sketch pad). Then, you very, very gently scribble on the paper, over where the coin is hidden beneath. I thought we could try coin-rubbing to help discover as much information about the coin as we possibly can."

"That's a great idea!" said Betty admiringly. "That's just the sort of technique that a professional historical detective or archaeologist might use. Here, pass me the wipes for now, though, and let's see if we can get this dirt and sand off to begin with."

Sophia handed the pack of baby wipes over to Betty and watched, fascinated, as her best friend ever-so carefully wiped away hundreds of years' worth of muck and grime to reveal a beautiful, gleaming, completely untarnished, shiny, gold-coloured coin.

"Wow" breathed both of the girls when the coin was cleaned up to its full glory. They were awe-struck at the beauty of the obviously pure gold treasure before them and they were bowled over by the thought that they really did have, in their possession, some real life pirate treasure.

"Can you make out anything on either of the coin's faces?" asked Sophia quietly and with somewhat bated breath.

"I think so," began Betty, as she strained, with the utmost concentration, to examine the coin. "It's not very easy to see exactly what the markings are, though. Oh, I know! Let's use the magnifying glasses from our go-bags, shall we, to see if that makes the engraving easier to see?!"

Extremely pleased to have a genuine excuse to use the magnifying glasses that they had been carrying around in their go-bags for weeks now, both girls took turns to examine the precious gold coin more closely. Betty looked intently at one side, before handing the coin over to allow Sophia to inspect the other.

"I think I can make out a person's head, with long curly hair, and I can just about feel with my fingertips, around the edge of the coin, what I think is some lettering, but I definitely can't read it. It's too small and unclear, even with the magnifying glass" said Betty.

"On this side I think I can see and feel some letters and numbers running in a circle around the edge, and there is some kind of intricate, decorative picture engraved in the centre. Shall we try the coin rubbing now to see if we can discover any more detail?" suggested Sophia.

Betty agreed immediately and, in turn, the girls very, very gently rubbed the soft drawing pencil over each of the paper-covered coin faces, to see whether the features which were engraved on the gold coin might be more clearly seen.

The girls' ingenuity and perseverance paid off as, bit by bit, the coin began to more distinctly reveal its secrets...

Chapter 14

"I was right" smiled Betty. "My side definitely shows what I'm pretty sure is a man's head with long curly hair. He also seems to be wearing some sort of headdress. There is some text, or letters or numbers, on one side, but it is simply too worn away for me to be able to read, either on the coin itself or on the rubbing. The text on the other side reads 'DEI. GRATIA'. I can read it, but I don't understand it. Is that a foreign language?"

"Yes, I think it must be. I don't recognise it," mused Sophia[6] "but I bet that will be really useful. In investigative terms, strange is good! The more unusual an object is, the more easily a detective can discover what it is or where it came from! We can probably look into coins showing that phrase and hopefully there won't be too many hits for us to wade through before we discover this coin's origins. I can also see from my coin rubbing that the picture in the centre is made up of what appear to be four small shields with different emblems on them, and each with a tiny crown at its top end. Most of the text is still completely indecipherable as far as I can see,

---

6   *'Dei gratia' is actually Latin and means 'by the grace of God'.*

but... yes! I can see a date! I can definitely read the date '1680'!"

"Brilliant!" cried Betty. "Late seventeenth century. Let's hit the books and the net, then shall we?! Surely the foreign phrase, the date and the pictures on either side of the coin will be enough to go on?!"

"I certainly hope so. Yes, let's get cracking with some more research. You know what, though, Betty?"

"What, Sophs?"

"We are literally holding in our hands, between the ship's log and the golden coin, actual, physical, certain, scientific, historical *proof* of the existence of treasure on Oak Island, of Sir Francis Drake's involvement *and* of a subsequent treasure burial too! This is amazing!"

Image credit: By Classical Numismatic Group, Inc. www.cngcoins.com, commons. wikimedia.org, Public Domain https://en.wikipedia.org/wiki/Guinea_(coin)#/media/ File:Guinea_641642.jpg

"I know!" nodded Betty feverishly. "It really is. People have been searching for proof like this for hundreds of years and we now actually have it. Gosh, Daniel and Anthony would be so, so pleased if they knew the value, never mind in terms of money but in historical worth, of what they had unearthed. Without access to libraries and the internet, though, the McGinnis treasure hunters would probably never have been able to find out just how important their discoveries really were, would they?"

So, with a real sense of the enormity of what they had already uncovered and how close they might well be to actually solving the real life history's mystery of the Oak Island treasure, the girls resumed their research once more.

The girls entered the search terms 'gold coin DEI.GRATIA emblem 1680' into their internet search engine and very quickly discovered that the exact coin that they were looking at was an English guinea from the reign of Charles II. The emblems which Sophia had spotted were actually the royal coats of arms of England (the Three Lions), Scotland (the Lion Rampant), France (the Fleur de Lis) and Ireland (the Harp).

This, however, is where things got a bit more tricky for our determined detective duo. The girls also learned from their wider reading that gold guineas were minted in all of the years from 1685 to 1688. Guineas were the main coin circulating in England and indeed across the whole of the British Empire during the late seventeenth century and even right up to the year 1816 (when guineas were eventually replaced by the pound that we know and use today). Sophia had been right: when you are conducting an investigation, strange or unusual is good. Incredibly common items, like this guinea once was, rarely point a detective to a definitive time, place, event or origin. Unfortunately for Sophia and Betty, therefore, the coin did not shed very much more light on how it had got to Oak Island and who on earth had buried it there after all.

Our intrepid amateur sleuths were not, however, easily deterred. Resilience is most certainly a quality which must be shared by investigators and treasure-hunters alike. So, a small set-back such as the worldwide prevalence of the 1680 gold guinea was not going to stop Sophia and Betty from solving the mystery of the Oak Island treasure – oh no! Instead, after a long afternoon of research, and a roller-coaster of a time-travelling day overall, the girls decided to take a break in which to clear their heads, and to rest and reinvigorate their little grey cells.

After carefully re-wrapping the ship's log and the gold coin in Betty's hoody and returning the priceless package to the relative safety of her go-bag, the girls grabbed a drink and a snack and burst out of the wooded den into the bright, warm, mid-afternoon sunshine. Quickly shaking off all thoughts of seventeenth century currency, wrecked ships and potential pirate perpetrators, and with Toby scampering and jumping delightedly around their feet, Sophia and Betty were very soon running around the garden with Ted and Reece, playing (and winning) a particularly serious game of boys v. girls football. Few things in life are more fun than beating little brothers at their own favourite games, and so, for the time being at least, the mystery of the Oak Island treasure would have to remain unsolved for just a little while longer.

Chapter 15

Sophia Slewfoot and Betty Babbington had made great strides towards solving the mystery of the Oak Island Treasure. They had time-travelled to the famous money pit in 1795 and had befriended treasure hunters, Daniel McGinnis and Anthony Vaughn. The girls had been given a ship's log which had been pulled from the pit and which seemed to confirm English explorer Sir Francis Drake's involvement in the construction of the pit and probably the burial of treasure. They had also been given a golden guinea from the late seventeenth century. It indicated that treasure had also been buried by another party, possibly as late as a century after Sir Francis Drake's death. Thereafter, their historical investigation had stalled.

The girls had spent a lovely hour playing with their brothers in Sophia's back garden, but were now keen to crack on with their case once more. They really hoped to solve the history's mystery before their rare and special day-long play date came to an end. So, when Sophia's mum asked the girls to take Toby for a quick walk before tea time, the girls leapt at the opportunity. A quick dog walk (which, with the magic of the marvellous PT machine could, of course, turn into an hours'-long or even days'-long trip!) could give them just the chance they needed to finally get to the bottom of the pirate treasure puzzle!

With their go-bags on their backs and with a pleased-as-punch Toby trotting at their feet, Sophia and Betty strode out into the warm and sunny late afternoon. They headed for the beautiful lakeside walk that was something of a tourist attraction within their pretty North West England village. Sophia and Betty knew that they were very lucky indeed to have such a renowned beauty spot as 'The Lake' on their doorstep, and they very much enjoyed walking and playing there whenever they got the chance. The wooded, waterside walk also boasted an ice-cream van, a hot drinks van and a pub with beer garden. The Lake was therefore always a buzzing and busy place for the girls to walk Tobes. It also afforded excellent opportunities for practising essential amateur sleuthing skills, such as people-watching, shadowing, note-taking, clue-finding and, for Toby, sniffing, tracking and protecting his precious mistress and her fantastic friend.

On this particular walk, however, the girls had no time for rehearsals. Absolutely not! This time it was the real thing! After allowing Toby a quick snuffle in the bushes and a rapid run around the lakeside path off his lead, the girls concentrated on finding a relatively quiet, out-of-the-way nook from which they could resume their time-travelling, history's mystery-solving mission!

Before too long, Sophia and Betty found the perfect place: an off-the-beaten-track rocky recess, set back slightly from the popular, well-trodden trail and veiled from view by dense undergrowth and overhanging, heavily-leaved branches. Setting themselves almost comfortably on the partially pebbly, partially pine needle covered ground, the girls settled in to a serious discussion about how on earth they were going to advance their Oak Island investigation.

"I'm afraid I don't think there's anything else for it, Sophs," declared Betty. "I think we simply need to time-travel back to Oak Island's pirate heyday, or there's a risk that we'll never learn anything more than we already know."

"I do agree," said Sophia slowly. "I feel sure that

we've ascertained all that we can from the ship's log, the golden guinea and our library books and internet research, but I'm still worried that we simply don't know *when exactly* to visit via the PT machine."

"Hmm," murmured Betty slowly and thoughtfully. "Let's analyse the evidence that we have gathered so far. We feel quite sure that the ship's log proves Sir Francis Drake's involvement, but the coin suggests that some treasure was also buried on Oak Island a long time after he had died. The coin was minted in 1680 in England. It would probably have been a good few years after that before it made its way outside of London and then travelled, by sea of course, perhaps to Europe, Africa, India or anywhere else in the world where English money would have been traded for silks, spices, porcelain, ivory, tea, coffee and more..."

"I see where you're going with this!" grinned Sophia admiringly. "Once the coin had been traded and had journeyed across the world, then it could have ended up on a ship which was captured by one of the many, many pirates that were operating in the seas during the late 1600s and early 1700s. That may have taken a further few years."

"Yes!" agreed Betty triumphantly, "And once a

pirate had amassed a fortune that he needed to hide, then it would have been a further few months or even a year or so before he ended up on Oak Island. Remember, travelling around the world took much, much longer in the olden days than it does now."

"Of course!" agreed Sophia. "So, if we take all that into account, how about we go back to visit Oak Island in, say, the year 1718? That's not quite forty years after the coin was minted (which is plenty of time for it to have made its way through numerous transactions throughout England and then around the trading Empire), and it's still around 10 to 15 years before the end of the Golden Age of Piracy."

"Why not?!" cried Betty excitedly. "That seems as sensible a date as any, so, yes! Let's do it!"

Pleased to have a plan once more, and eager to travel back in time to visit Oak Island again, Sophia carefully pulled the PT machine out of her go-bag. She looped the handle of the PT machine and Toby's lead through her belt hooks and tied herself and Betty together with the strong, long rope that Anthony Vaughn had kindly given to them to enable them to more freely (but still safely) move around while they were time-travelling. Sophia then began to turn the hands of the PT machine to the date they wished to visit – early 1718.

As the girls had already travelled to Oak Island at the outset of their inquiry, Sophia felt quite confident that she could remember exactly how to set the PT machine's coordinates hands so that they would arrive in exactly the same spot as before. What neither Sophia nor Betty realised, however, was that when Sophia was turning and setting the delicate coordinates hands which determined the location to which the PT machine would take the time-travellers, she actually, accidentally placed the latitude hand just a degree or so off where she intended to, and...

Whooshkazzamflashzingwow!!!

Before the girls noticed their mistake, they were gone.

Chapter 16

"Erm, Sophs," began Betty, somewhat nervously, after the jolt, thwack and flash of PT machine-time travel had subsided. "Where are we?"

"I, uh, hmm," stuttered Sophia. "I, I don't know. I don't recognise this place. Oh dear, has something gone wrong?"

"I thought that we would arrive on Oak Island in the same spot as last time," said Betty "but this place looks completely different."

Betty was right. As both girls took a few moments to survey their surroundings it became very clear indeed that they had not arrived where they had intended. In fact, the girls could not even tell whether they had landed on Oak Island at all, or whether they had ended up in some other, unfamiliar and as yet unidentified location. Actually, Sophia's inadvertent error when setting the PT machine's coordinates had meant that the girls and Toby had time-travelled, not to Oak Island, but to one of the many harsh, uninhabited, rocky outcrop islands that peppered Mahone Bay, and which were generally too dangerous and too desolate for any person to visit.

The setting in which the girls now found themselves was a harsh, rocky coastline, where cruel-looking, black, jagged rocks rose up out of the surf and the shore, like the spiky, sharp teeth of a snarling shark. The rocks were being lashed ferociously by the churning, roiling, battering, foamy ocean. Instead of a gently rising wooded path leading from a sandy cove into the centre of the island, huge, sheer, dark cliffs loomed ahead of the increasingly concerned Sophia, Betty and Toby as they turned to view the island's terrain. As they took in their surroundings and tried to assess the situation, deafening waves continued to crash and smash menacingly behind them, roaring like an angry beast and contributing to the girls' growing sense of unease. Toby, too, could feel that something was wrong, very wrong. He was quivering with fear and anxiety, his limbs were taught with tension, his hackles were standing right up on end and he was prowling round and round the girls' feet. It was as if he knew that he needed to guard and protect the girls, but he didn't know from whom, what or where any potential threat might come.

Never before in any of Sophia's time-travelling, history's mysteries adventures had our brave historical heroine felt such a deep-seated fear and concern about the place and time in which she had found herself. But dread and worry were what Sophia felt now. She knew that something had gone awry with their time-travelling experience and, as keen as she was to solve the mystery of the Oak Island treasure, she didn't want her best friend, her beloved Tobes, or herself to be in genuine danger for even a single second. Sophia was therefore just about to re-set the date and co-ordinates hands on the PT machine back to the safety of the real life present day and the girls' home village when, all of a sudden, Betty grabbed her harshly by the arm and pulled her, forcibly, to the floor.

"Wh, what...?" Sophia started to say, but Betty interrupted her.

"Shhh!! Sophia, be quiet! Look!"

Betty jerked her head towards the cliff face just a little way along the rocky shore from where the girls and Tobes were now lying, huddled together and pressed against the damp and gravelly ground. Sophia followed with her eyes in the direction Betty had indicated and she saw, with a shock, what appeared to be the entrance to a cave in the craggy cliffs. Coming out of the cave was, no – it couldn't be, but yes, it was! A pirate! An actual, authentic, large-as-life, genuine, real life pirate! Oh my goodness me, and a terrifying one at that.

The spot where Sophia, Betty and Toby were lying, pushing themselves as closely into the sharp, rocky sand as they possibly could, was actually, thankfully, hidden from the pirate's line of sight. As the shore rose upwards from where the girls and Toby had unceremoniously flung themselves to the floor, the pirate, if he had glanced in their direction, would only have seen the rocky brow which rose slightly, mercifully, just ahead of them. Nevertheless, the girls and Tobes were in an incredibly uncomfortable and exposed situation, and one in which they would definitely be seen if the pirate should decide to walk even just a few steps closer to the ocean's edge. The girls knew instinctively that, the second the pirate turned his back, they needed to make a run for cover.

One benefit of the harsh, jagged landscape in which they had found themselves was that there were lots of huge, slimy, barnacle-covered boulders jutting out of the gravelly ground and rising up around them. Speaking to each other silently with their eyes (as only best friends and much-loved pets can do) Sophia, Betty and Toby agreed that, as soon as the pirate's back was fully turned, all three of them would make a dash for it, to hide behind the nearest boulder.

With their hearts hammering hard in their chests, with the sounds of both the incessant ocean and their own persistent pulse pumping in their ears, and with their hands clasped together and around Toby's short lead, the girls watched and waited. Then, immediately the opportunity presented itself, all three leaped up and pelted towards the welcome dark cover of the big, black rock before them.

It was, unfortunately, impossible for the girls and Toby to move across the rocky beach without their feet disturbing the gravel and pebbles beneath them. It was excruciating to hear what they were sure was the thunderously loud crunch of their footsteps as they ran. For a heart-stopping moment, while they stooped behind their rocky shield, the girls felt sure that the pirate had heard them and was on his way to confront them. To their immense relief, however, just as the pirate turned to see what had suddenly made a scuffling, crunching sound behind him, a flock of seagulls fluttered up off the gritty ground and flew away overhead. The pirate watched the gulls fly away and seemed satisfied that they had caused the kerfuffle.

From their hidden vantage point, Sophia and Betty finally allowed themselves to take a breath and to relax a little. They turned, then, to scrutinise the pirate, not through the eyes of two frightened ten year old girls, but instead with the keen observation of two serious and practised amateur sleuths. What they saw was shocking indeed.

The pirate was huge! He seemed to be an absolute giant of a man. His height was no doubt exaggerated by the fact that he wore enormous, heeled, black leather boots with wicked-looking pointy toes and a large overturned flap beneath the man's knees. He also wore a massive, black, tattered tricorn hat with an evil, cackling skull and crossbones on the front. Quite apart from the giant's size, the pirate was terrifying-looking because of the moustache and fearsome, bushy, long black beard which hid most of his face from view and reached down his chest, almost to the man's waist, where it was twisted and gnarled into a mass of matted dreadlocks. Even worse, falling out from under the tatty tricorn hat, was the pirate's jet black, greasy, knotted hair. Much of that was also wound into dishevelled dreadlocks. Horrifyingly, the locks of hair which immediately framed the right and left side of the pirate's face had lighted tapers entwined within them, giving the impression that the man himself was spouting fiery, lethal flames. With the hat, the hair, the moustache and the mammoth, wild, unkempt beard, the only part of the pirate's face that was at all visible was his eyes. And what ghastly, chilling eyes they were too. The pirate's eyes were drawn wide and rolled and darted around in an unsettling, highly disconcerting manner. It seemed that no matter where a person might be, the pirate's constantly darting, unblinking and crazed eyes would surely find them.

All in all, the pirate's size, appearance and overall demeanour created the unmistakeable impression of volatility, horror, and evil. Sophia, Betty and Toby were scared stiff.

Chapter 17

From their perilous hiding place behind a fortuitously placed boulder on the unforgiving, rocky beach on which, due to Sophia's error in setting the coordinates, the PT machine had landed our daring amateur detectives, Sophia and Betty had watched in shock and fear as a an enormous and horrendously frightening real life pirate had emerged from a concealed cave in the cliff face. After watching the pirate for several minutes, and having satisfied themselves that they were safely out of his sightline for the time being, the girls finally dared turn to each other and to discuss the predicament in which they found themselves.

"Oh Sophs, what on earth are we going to do?!" moaned Betty. "That pirate looks absolutely wicked and vile. We absolutely cannot let him see us. I'd bet he'd kill us for sure!"

"He does look completely horrifying," agreed Sophia, "but something's ringing a bell in the back of my mind. Something that I read right at the outset of our investigation, I think, when we hit the library first thing this morning. Oh, I wish I could remember what it was!"

"Really?" asked Betty incredulously. "Is it something that you think could help us get out of here?!"

"No, no. I'm not actually worried about getting away, Bets," reassured Sophia, now that she had had a few moments to catch her breath and to collect her thoughts. "We can always get away in an instant if we need to, look". Sophia gently turned the face of the PT machine, which remained strapped to her belt, towards Betty. "I can set the PT machine in just a second to our home time and date to enable us to make an immediate get-away if ever that horrible pirate turns this way and starts to come towards us. No, that's not what's bugging me. Oh, I wish I could put my finger on it!"

"Ok, well maybe I can help you" suggested Betty. "I'll talk you through what we were reading in the library, step-by-step, and hopefully that will help you to remember what you're trying to bring to mind. It's a classic recall hack, often used by detectives when they are interviewing witnesses. So, hmm, if I remember correctly, we had spoken to Miss Reading. She had helped us to find some books. We were learning about Oak Island generally; the types of treasure that have been found so far; theories behind the mystery; the Golden Age of Piracy; Captain William Kidd; the many, many pirates that were operating across the seas..."

"Yes! That's it!" cried Sophia, in a whisper that was actually a little too loud and a little too excited for the girls' current, very precarious, position.

"What's it?!" asked Betty, anxiously but also somewhat impatiently.

"While I was reading about Captain Kidd and all of the other pirates that famously operated in the 1600s and 1700s, I read about a particularly notorious pirate called *Blackbeard*." As Sophia spoke the name she lowered her voice to such a quiet whisper that Betty had to really strain to hear her. Sophia continued: "Blackbeard plundered ships and petrified his victims in a relatively short but severe reign over the seas between England, North America and the Caribbean, I think. I saw some pictures of him in some of the library books and on the internet, and they showed his dreadlocked hair and beard. Most importantly, I remember reading that Blackbeard often lit wicks in his hair to make him appear other-worldly and even more terrifying than any other pirate alive."

"OMG!" whimpered Betty. "The most terrifying pirate alive? And that's him? Right in front of us, just over there?!"

"Well yes, I think that's him," started Sophia, "but the thing is, while he may have *appeared* to have been the most terrifying pirate of the day, in actual fact he wasn't really that much of a baddie."

"He wasn't that much of a baddie?!" marvelled Betty. "What the flippin' heck do you mean by that, Sophs?! Have you gone mad?! He's a massive, scary, robbing, murderous, outlaw, pirate, isn't he, or, wasn't he?!"

"Well, I read that, in fact, while he was an incredibly fearsome raider and thief, famed for ransacking ship after ship, making many, many enemies and amassing huge stores of booty as a result, he actually wasn't very violent at all. It seems that Blackbeard relied upon his shocking, horrifying appearance and his reputation as a crazed madman, to the extent that he almost never had to resort to killing or even really hurting anyone. Instead, most of the time, victims just immediately backed down whenever he was around, and he walked away with the loot without ever doing too much real harm to anyone."

"Wow, that's great recollection, Sophs, and actually some quite reassuring research. I don't think I really want to put it to the test, though, do you? I still think that, to be on the safe side, we should keep ourselves completely out of Blackbeard's sight while we're on this awful, rocky outcrop of an island."

Sophia was about to agree with her best friend and fellow historical sleuth when, all of a sudden, Toby's hackles began to stand up on end once more. Toby also started to emit a quiet but menacing growling sound, which the girls recognised as signalling potential danger.

Slowly, carefully, Sophia and Betty inched their heads around the side of the boulder behind which they were hiding, to try to see what was concerning their faithful and protective pooch.

The girls were amazed to see that Blackbeard was being joined, via a small-ish wooden boat that had somehow managed to negotiate the crashing waves and the lethal jagged coastline and was now being pulled up on to the rocky shore, by yet another pirate! This man was much less scary-looking. He was wearing torn and weathered early eighteenth-century peasant-type clothes and was really only marked out as a pirate by the skull and crossbones flag that was flapping from a small mast at the bow of his boat.

The girls' amazement increased even further, and their eyes widened in excitement and glee, when they realised the purpose of this lesser pirate's rendezvous with the infamous Blackbeard... It was a treasure transfer!

Chapter 18

As Sophia and Betty watched, crouched behind the sole rock which shielded them from the view of two real life eighteenth century pirates, one of whom had gone down in history as one of the most disreputable and frightening pirates the world had ever known, the two men started to unload, from the rickety wooden boat that had recently arrived on shore, a cache of treasure the like of which Sophia and Betty could never, ever have imagined.

Sack after sack after sack, each one overflowing with gold and silver coins, was being passed out of the boat by the smaller, scruffier pirate, and were being taken into the cave by the imposing, domineering Blackbeard. Once the sacks full of coinage had been unloaded, box after chest after box after chest of jewels, silver plate[7], gold bullion[8], precious metals and shimmering silks were also

---

7   *Silver plate is a collective term which refers to plates, bowls, dishes, cutlery, candlesticks – all manner of tableware – that is coated in silver.*

8   *Gold bullion is a term used to describe the precious metal gold when it has been formed into solid bars and proven to meet high, recognised standards of quality and purity.*

transported from the shaky and shabby boat into the depths of what was obviously a deep, dark cavern.

The girls were transfixed. They watched, almost breathless, as the extraordinary hoard was unpacked by the second, raggedy pirate, and then inspected and hidden away by Blackbeard. Sophia and Betty had read a lot about the Golden Age of Piracy and they had seen pictures of treasure chests in books and online, but they simply couldn't have conceived, even in their wildest dreams, the beauty and brilliance of the bounty that was now before them.

Against the rough, dark and grim backdrop of the harsh island on which they had accidentally landed, the treasure seemed to glisten and glow all the more; with gold, silver, platinum, diamonds, rubies, emeralds, sapphires, pearls and more, all shimmering, shining and glinting, brightening up the otherwise pale and dreary late afternoon light.

The hoard that the pirates were unloading would surely have been worth an absolute fortune, even back in 1718. In the present day, however, the value of the treasure would have been priceless in the very truest sense of the word. Every single precious item would have increased exponentially in value over time in any event. Then, with the added extra value occasioned by the fact that this was genuine pirate treasure and was of untold historical significance, well, Sophia and Betty simply couldn't even begin to comprehend the importance and full worth of what they were witnessing before their very eyes.

After several, mesmerising minutes of watching the pirates unload, inspect and transport the treasure to the cave, Sophia finally managed to tear her eyes away from the spectacular scene, and to whisper a few words to Betty.

"Gosh, Bets, can you believe what we are seeing?! How unbelievably amazing is this?! I don't know about you, but I don't even feel at all scared any more. I am just so bowled over by the sight of all that booty, that I just feel so, so excited and lucky and happy that we time-travelled to this island instead of to Oak Island after all!"

"I know, me too!" breathed Betty, elatedly. This has literally been the best play date *ever*!!!"

"Just think," said Sophia softly and somewhat in wonderment. "We set off on an adventure this morning to try to solve the mystery of the treasure thought to have been left on Oak Island by Captain Kidd, but we have actually ended up witnessing another pirate, the notorious Blackbeard, red-handedly hiding another priceless hoard on a neighbouring island. We weren't really focusing on reading about Blackbeard this morning, but I seem to recall that no one has ever found his treasure either, partly because no one was ever even sure where to look. Perhaps we have inadvertently stumbled upon and solved another pirate treasure mystery instead?!"

Chapter 19

Before Betty could respond, however, the girls' attention was grabbed by the sound of the formidable Blackbeard suddenly barking some instructions to his subordinate. In a rough, gravelly, English West Country accent, Blackbeard growled "All right then, lad, that'll do I reckon. That's the lot of it. You set to work a-blockin' up that there cavern-mouth now, while I have m'self a smoke."

With that, Blackbeard sat himself down on a flat-ish rock at the side of the entrance to the cave, stretched out his legs before him and leaned to rest his back against the sheer cliff face. Sophia and Betty watched, wide-eyed as he proceeded to light a pipe from the fire burning at the end of one of his knotty dreadlocks, and to smoke it with a very smug, self-satisfied air. He turned to speak to his shipmate. "You, me hearty, be the only mate alive who knows where me booty's buried. You'd better keep it that way! If you keep yer big mouth shut, I'll make it worth yer while, lad! Oh yes, you and me'll be two of the richest buccaneers on earth for the rest of our days, so we will! If, however, ye ever breathe a word of this to *any* other man, woman or child alive, then I'll slit yer throat from ear t'ear, bounce yer bonce off the bow of me biggest boat, and the man, woman or child ye told'll be next! D'ye hear me?! D'ye savvy?! Aye, I tell ye, a loyal mate can live a long and wealthy life and dead men tell no tales. Remember both of them truths and ye'll do well. Forget, and blab about me booty, and that'll be the *death* of ye, so it will!"

"Aye, aye Capt'n, me lips are sealed, I swear it, cross me heart and cross me bones!" the other pirate solemnly replied.

"Good lad, good lad," nodded Blackbeard, seemingly gratified with his mate's assurances. "Right then, just one last thing. Walk me through exactly how ye left things at the pit. We can then call it a night and get off this hellish, evil island. The luxury and comforts of me Captain's cabin aboard the Queen Anne's Revenge are a-callin', but I need to know that we've finished our lootin' in this 'ere Mahone Bay."

"Righty-ho, Capt'n" said the second pirate, puffing out his chest importantly and beginning to brief his boss on the day's pillaging and plundering. "Well Sir, I went right down as far as I possibly could into the bottom of that there pit. The shaft was shored up all around with huge wooden beams and there were step ladders and ropes affixed to 'em, so it wasn't too difficult to climb down. Every now 'n then there was a wooden platform built into the side of the shaft. A real feat of engineerin', like nothin' I've ever seen before, Sir. On each and every one of them platforms was some of these 'ere treasure chests and sacks. Some of 'em near the top were filled with silks and spices and the like, but the deeper down into the pit I descended, the more precious the booty seemed to get! Suddenly the chests were stuffed with sacks of gold 'n' silver coins, seemingly from all over the Empire! Some of the sacks were bulging with hundreds and hundreds of them there gold doubloons, which even I knows were robbed from them pesky Spanish back when they tried (and failed!) to invade our God's own country."

"Ha ha haaaggghhh" half-laughed, half-growled Blackbeard, in an almost maniacal manner. "We've not just pilfered ol' Kidd's pirate plunder, then, so we haven't! No, we've hit the jackpot matey! We've found ol' Drakey's personal private stash, so we have! He's the one what looted all them fine Spanish vessels and I always knew he wouldn't-a handed it all over to his fancy lady Queen! Woo hoo hoo, first-rate plunder-pinching! All right, then what next, m'laddie, what next?"

The pirate was puffing and panting as he heaved rocks and boulders into place, to obscure and secure the mouth of the cave, but he continued: "Well, after a while, the further down I reached, into the deepest, darkest depths of that horrible, gaping, hell-hole of a pit, the more it started fillin' and a-fillin' with water. The lowest platform that I could find was empty too, other than bits and bobs of ol' diggin' and a-buildin' gear. Ye know the stuff, tools and shovels and raggedly ol' ropes and the like. The platform just one level above that last 'un was where a strange piece of loot was stashed. It's, er, it's this one 'ere Sir. You've not inspected it yet as, erm, I've just remembered sire, I, um, I stuffed it in me sack so as, erm, so as not to lose it, yes, so as not to lose it. It's a little one see, so it is."

Handing over a quite small wooden chest (with the guilty air of a man who had been contemplating double-crossing his menacing master but then thought better of it at the last minute), the pirate went on: "After I'd snatched up this 'ere hardwood box – heavier than it looks, so it is – I figured that, what with the sea-water soakin' in and the hoard havin' dried up at those depths, I must-a got to the bottom there, and I must-a grabbed and nicked every last scrap worth pinchin'!"

Eyeing his subordinate shrewdly, Blackbeard snarled "Aye, I'm sure ye've grabbed the lot, matey, I'm sure ye have. Ye'll know what'll happen to ye if I find out that ye're a-lyin- to me or a-double-crossin'! So, I'll take yer word for it and we'll get rich off all of this lot, that's for sure. But ye're right, m'laddie, ye're right. We haven't checked the contents of this 'ere coffer yet have we?! Let's do it now, me hearty, let's get in now to that there box!"

With that, the huge, half-crazed, half-gleeful Blackbeard, smashed his sword (a massive, curved cutlass which, until this point had been sheathed at his side, hanging from his filthy, shabby cummerbund) down hard on to the one box which the pirates had not yet opened and inspected. The wood shattered and shards flew in all directions, causing the girls to jump out of their skins, and then to panic for a few seconds that they had given themselves away. Inside the wooden outer casing, the box was constructed out of what appeared to be a strong, heavy metal of some sort. ('Perhaps lead, to protect whatever is inside?' thought Sophia to herself.) Even that was no match for the fierce and powerful pirate captain. With one more crashing slam of his sword, the clanging shriek of metal on metal slicing through the ever-present thundering of breakers crashing on the shore, Blackbeard burst open the fascinating final little box.

"Woo hoo hoo!" cooed Blackbeard again, greedily this time. "What do we have 'ere, then, me hearty?!"

From their uncomfortable but hidden perch behind a boulder on the rocky beach, Sophia and Betty craned their necks to see what the pirates had discovered inside the mysterious chest. Even Toby seemed to pick up on a sense of growing excitement. Alarmingly, he began to inch and sniff towards where Blackbeard was about to unveil the box's contents. Luckily, as Toby's lead was still tethered tightly to Sophia's belt, she felt a gentle tug as the inquisitive Beagle started to edge towards the pirates, and she was able to yank, quickly but quietly, on the lead. Sophia managed to pull Toby back into the safety of their hiding place just in the nick of time, before he gave them all away!

As Blackbeard and his ship-mate were so engrossed in their inspection of the last vestiges of their loot, the girls were able to edge around the boulder behind which they were hiding just enough to give themselves a relatively clear view. They watched, almost spellbound, as the pirates lifted what appeared to be a folded flag out of the little wooden box.

The pirates roughly discarded the flag and threw it towards where the girls were crouching. The flag landed just a few steps away, close enough for the girls to see that the flag was embroidered with the repeated image of a symbol. The girls knew that they had seen the emblem before, but they couldn't, in the moment, quite place it. Sophia slowly and silently pulled a notebook and pen from her go-bag and did a quick sketch:

The girls knew that they could always check the symbol with some quick research later. It might just be an historical clue as to the origins of this obviously very special treasure!

The next minute the girls heard a great big booming belly-laugh bellow out from the fearsome Blackbeard. "Whoa ho ho, ha ha ha!" he cried. "Look at these gems and jewels and pearls and rings and crowns and all sorts of bedazzling booty! What a prize! I've never seen pickin's as posh 'n' pricey as these! Oooh, aye, I reckon this 'ere last little box has surely given us our most pretty and precious pile yet, so it has!"

From what the girls could see, Blackbeard was absolutely right. Although Sophia and Betty couldn't catch a glimpse of all the contents of the special chest, they could make out jewellery, gemstones and even a tiny but breathtakingly beautiful diamond-encrusted tiara, all of which were more spectacular than any of the other magnificent treasures that they had seen so far on this astonishing historical adventure. The tiara, in particular, was glinting and glowing so much that it was as if the evening's silvery light was emanating from the diamonds themselves, rather than from the moon which had just begun to shine in the dusky sky overhead. It was very clear to Sophia and Betty that the last little chest contained treasure that was truly special indeed.

Chapter 20

All the while Blackbeard had been bashing away at the last wooden box and then fawning over its contents, the second pirate had been blocking up the entrance to the cave in which Sir Francis Drake's and Captain Kidd's re-stolen stashes had now been stored. By the time Blackbeard had finished chuckling to himself about his good luck in stealing such an impressive and valuable cache from the Oak Island money pit, there was just enough of the cavern entrance left clear for the boisterous, treasure-grabbing brute to roughly chuck into the cave the precious little box, before finally closing the cave up altogether. In spite of themselves, the girls were impressed. All of a sudden it was if the cave simply didn't exist. Instead, the mound of rocks at the foot of the cliff appeared, to the unknowing eye, to be nothing more than a pile of scree, that was barely discernible amongst the rocky cliffs and the grey, stony, gravelly ground. Sophia and Betty felt the full force of the knowledge that, if they had not accidentally landed on this harsh and uninhabited island and witnessed, with their own eyes, the re-hiding of this priceless pirates' loot, it may well never have been found by anyone throughout history ever again.

"Come on then, matey!" Blackbeard yelled. "We're a-gettin' off this scraggy old lump o' rock now and we're a-headin' back to the Queen Anne! On the way, though, m'laddie, we're goin' to throw back down into that stinkin' pit just a few of these doubloons and this one glintin' trinket that I've pilfered from that last coffer." At that, Blackbeard held up a beautiful bright red jewel set in a shining gold, oval-shaped, engraved and bejewelled surround.

It was truly lovely, but from what Sophia and Betty had seen, they knew that it was one of the lesser treasures that had been wrapped in the old flag and hidden in the now smashed-to-smithereens lead-lined box.

"Aarrgghh, ha ha ha! That'll confound anyone who ever tries to come a-lookin' for all that treasure!" cackled Blackbeard. "We'll leave it so that they find just enough to keep 'em a-huntin' at old Oak Island! Ha ha ha, ho ho, never'll come the day when any ol' pilferin' picaroon thinks to – ooh, ha ha ha – thinks to look on this nasty, gnarled rock just, he he he, just right next door!"

Sophia watched, wide-eyed, as Blackbeard screeched with glee at his, admittedly very clever (and, as history would show, actually very successful), plan to leave what Sophia now understood to be *decoy* treasure at Oak Island. The idea, which had actually worked perfectly in accordance with Blackbeard's plan, was to keep any future treasure-hunters' attention on Oak Island and away from the location where he had actually hidden the stupendous stash that he had stolen from that very place.

Sophia realised that she and Betty had now solved the mystery of the Oak Island treasure after all! The answer was that the treasure had been buried by earlier pirates such as Sir Francis Drake and probably Captain Kidd, but then pinched, thereafter, by Blackbeard. That scurvy rascal had then hidden it away on this neighbouring island, and deliberately left just sufficient scraps of treasure in the Oak Island pit to keep hunters throughout history hooked on searching in what was actually the wrong place!

Sophia turned to share her revelations with Betty but was shocked to see that her friend was in the process of reaching out, as far as she could from behind the boulder that was concealing them, to try to grab the old flag which Blackbeard had flung away. To Sophia's horror, as her friend stretched and strained to try to grab the flag without leaving the shelter of their rock, Betty over-balanced. She tumbled, head first and with a hideously loud, rocky, crunchy crash, into the pebbly shore, *straight* into the full sight of Blackbeard himself!

The initial surprise in Blackbeard's beady black eyes quickly turned to rage as he saw Betty, Sophia and Toby, who were all tied together and trying to run away, but kept slipping and sliding and crunching and crashing into each other and into the sharp, slimy and shingly shore. It had dawned on Blackbeard that the location of his stash was no longer secret and that his masterplan to use the Oak Island pit as a decoy had been discovered, and by two silly little girls at that! Blackbeard was *fuming* and he bellowed in fury as he charged, with all his massive might, sword drawn and eyes ablaze, towards the terrified trio.

With her heart pounding and her fingers fumbling, Sophia somehow just about managed to move the hands of the PT machine back to the date, time and place that she knew so well – the girls' real life present day and their home village. Just then, and just, *just*, in the nick of time, there was a brilliant...

Whooshkazzamflashzingwow!!!

and the girls were gone.

Chapter 21

Phew!!! That had been a bit too close for comfort. Sophia and Betty had had an unbelievably exciting and successful day. They had solved the mystery of the Oak Island treasure that had baffled treasure-hunters and historians alike for hundreds of years, but they had also almost come a cropper. Through an accident of time- and place- travel with the amazing PT machine, the girls had inadvertently come face-to-face with Blackbeard, one of the most menacing pirates of all time. They had just about managed to escape the clutches of the crazed pirate after they had discovered that he had stolen treasure which had been buried at Oak Island during the sixteenth and seventeenth centuries, and that he had re-hidden it on a neighbouring island, leaving behind on Oak Island only a few tantalising trinkets as a decoy.

For a good minute or two after arriving back to the safety of their sheltered spot alongside the beautiful lakeside path in the real life present day, Sophia, Betty and Toby simply sat, stunned, trying to take in all that had happened to them that day.

Then, rousing herself with a deep breath and a

decisive shake of the head, Sophia turned to Betty and started to speak about their amazing adventure.

"Bets! We did it! We solved the mystery of the Oak Island Treasure!"

"Yes, and we escaped with our lives – just about!" agreed Betty with a wide-eyed, and somewhat relieved, grin.

"I know" agreed Sophia. "Blackbeard was *cross* when he realised that we had discovered his hiding place and his decoy plan."

"Hmm, you know what, though, Sophs" mused Betty. "We left that neighbouring island in such a hurry in the end that we actually don't know whether Blackbeard felt confident enough to leave his secret stash hidden there, or whether he moved it again, to another location. If he did move it, worrying that we might reveal his secret and steal his treasure, then the hoard will have actually been lost to history all over again. Wouldn't that be a shame?"

"Yes it would, Bets, but, you know what, I don't think that Blackbeard did move the treasure again."

"You don't think he did?" asked Betty. "Why not? What makes you think that?"

"Well, just imagine. Two little girls and a dog from

140

the future suddenly appearing out of nowhere on an uninhabited island in the Atlantic Ocean, and then disappearing without trace in the blink of an eye! That will surely have seemed so strange and so incongruous to Blackbeard that I reckon he must have doubted whether he had really ever seen us at all. I think it is probably more likely that he will have ultimately assumed that he must have been seeing things. Just think about it. Blackbeard won't have known anything about us or the PT machine, so he can't possibly have realised what had actually happened. I bet he ended up having to conclude that we were just a figment of his imagination. Plus, of course, we do have some evidence..."

"Evidence?" queried Betty. "What do you mean?"

"Well, we know that people have been hunting for treasure on Oak Island for years and years and, of course, they have found some of the decoy trinkets that we know Blackbeard deliberately threw back down into the pit!" At this, Sophia grabbed her tablet and pulled up a website which listed some of the treasures that have been found on Oak Island throughout history. Included in that list were a jewelled brooch and Spanish coins, exactly like the items which Sophia and Betty knew that Blackbeard had intended to leave behind, to foil future treasure-hunters.

"Oh yes, you're right, Sophs!" beamed Betty. "That's fantastic sleuthing! So, we've definitely solved the mystery, but, well, what do we do now?! Do we tell everyone? Do we somehow organise a real life treasure-hunt in the right place? Do we even know exactly where the right place actually is? We landed there entirely by mistake, remember, so did we even make a note of those co-ordinates? If we do find the treasure, do we get to keep it?! Will we be rich?!?!"

"Whoa, whoa, slow down, Bets!" laughed Sophia. "No, no, just think for a minute. We can't go telling everyone what we've discovered without also having to tell them *how*. If we mention any of this to anyone, we'll have to reveal the existence of the PT machine, and I really don't want to do that. My mum and dad would go *mad* if they knew that we'd been time- and place- travelling. They'd take the PT machine away and ground me for sure."

Betty nodded slowly as the reality of the situation sank in.

Sophia continued: "No, I'm sorry, but I really think

that we need to keep all of this to ourselves and I don't think we can ever get rich as a result of finding the treasure. I'm pretty sure that we can't arrange recovery of the hoard without help. Even if we were able to return to the secret cave and somehow tether all of the heavy treasure to the PT machine to try to bring it back to the present day, we could never show, or sell, or spend, or do *anything* with the treasure without exposing our secrets. So, all in all, I think we'll just have to be quietly and privately content with the satisfaction that comes with solving one of history's greatest mysteries – just like I was when I solved the mystery of the Mary Celeste. It does seem a real shame, though. Just think of how valuable the treasure would be to archaeologists, historians, museum curators, teachers..."

As Sophia tailed off somewhat mournfully, Betty jumped in with a worrying thought which had, just that moment, occurred to her.

"It's not just about the historical worth actually, Sophs, what about the curse of Oak Island? Isn't it going to go on claiming the lives of hunters who put themselves at risk in that horrible, dangerous pit for so long as the treasure remains unfound? I know that we are not supposed to interfere with history, but now that we know the truth, are we not under a moral responsibility to make sure that no more lives are lost?"

"Gosh, Bets, you might be on to something!" agreed Sophia. "I'm sure we did a good thing stopping the McGinnis party from continuing to hunt for treasure and we may therefore have saved their lives. Perhaps we should do something to prevent any future fatal accidents too. But what?"

"Ooh, ooh, I've got a plan, Sophs, I've got a plan!" cried Betty suddenly, jumping up and down in excitement. Sophia had to remind her to keep her voice down, in case any passing dog walkers or tourists were able to overhear any of their top secret discussions.

"Although it would have been very nice indeed for us to keep the ship's log and gold guinea that Daniel McGinnis gave to us, you are correct, Sophs, that we could never do anything with them, other than merely keep them as a memento of our adventure. That would be a bit of a waste, really, especially when you think about what real, grown-up, professional, history experts could learn from such precious artefacts. Plus, of course, we've still got our coin-rubbings. They're a great souvenir in themselves, aren't they? So, how about we send the log and the coin to, oh, I don't know, the British Museum perhaps? We could even send them wrapped up in this, in case it is another clue." At this, Betty produced from her go-bag the tattered old flag which Blackbeard had discarded in his haste to inspect the contents of the last little treasure chest.

"Wow, Bets, that's a really brilliant idea!" said Sophia, impressed. We could include an anonymous note to point the museum's experts (and probably the press and modern-day treasure-hunters the world over!) in the right direction. We'd just need to hint that the Oak Island treasure is out there, but on one of the *neighbouring* islands in Mahone Bay."

"Yes!" nodded Betty decisively. "Let's do just that! We can then sit back and enjoy watching real life experts discover, recover, learn from and display the treasure. That will allow the world at large the opportunity to enjoy and benefit from the treasure! It won't remain trapped in its hidden rocky prison any longer and the myth of the Oak Island pit won't claim any more lives! Oh let's do it, Sophs, lets!"

And so, to finish off what was surely one of the best, most exciting and, at times, most hair-raising play dates of all time, the two happy little girls, and Tobes of course, raced back to Sophia's house to draft an anonymous note and to package up their exceedingly precious parcel. What's more, thanks to the magic of the PT machine, Sophia and Betty were home from their 'dog walk' (!) just in time for a lovely fish 'n' chip tea – perfect!

Although it was too late to make the last post of the day, Sophia was confident that her mum would allow her to pop down to the Post Office in the village the next day, where Sophia would be sure to arrange a 'Special Delivery' (and it would be special indeed!) to the British Museum. Thereafter, the girls would just have to wait...

OAK ISLAND MYTH MIX-UP!

A treasure-hunting expedition backed by the British Museum has unearthed what experts believe to be the legendary Oak Island treasure... but not on Oak Island!

Ms Anne Tiquity, Chief Curator of Historical Artefacts at the British Museum explains: "It was the strangest thing. Just a few months ago, the Museum received an unmarked package containing some incredibly interesting and authentic, but historically disparate items: the ship's log from the Nuestra Señora del Rosario, one of the ships of the Spanish Armada captured by Sir Francis Drake in 1588; a golden guinea from the British Empire, dated 1680; and a pre-Revolution French flag embroidered with a 'Fleur de Lis' emblem.

Our conservators dated the flag to around 1789, and traced it to the court of King Louis XVI. There was also a handwritten note, which the author had made to appear as if it had been written by a child, obviously in an attempt to maintain anonymity and to evade discovery via our expert graphologists. The note suggested that the Oak Island treasure existed and was waiting to be discovered, but that it was hidden in a rocky cave on a neighbouring island in Mahone Bay, and not on Oak Island itself. Well, with such specific information, and with the exceptional corroborating evidence of the already fascinating and historically priceless artefacts which accompanied the note, the British Museum was only too pleased to mount an expedition to locate the treasure. We are very, very pleased indeed to be able to confirm today that the expedition was a resounding success!"

Experts have confirmed that the treasure which has now been recovered from an uninhabited rocky outcrop just a few hundred metres across the bay from the famous Oak Island, is one of the most historically significant discoveries ever made. The cache contains items dating back to the 1500s which have been confirmed to originate in expeditions under the charge of the oft-revered but also somewhat controversial figure, Sir Francis Drake. It also contains treasure which can be attributed to at least two notorious bandits from the Golden Age of Piracy, Captain William Kidd and Edward Teach AKA Blackbeard. Perhaps most exciting of all, several items discovered within this remarkable haul have been verified as being the remaining priceless pieces from the collection of French crown jewels, which once belonged to King Louis XVI and Marie-Antoinette, but which disappeared mysteriously amid the chaos of the royal family's attempt to flee the French Revolution.

In terms of what this varied and prized treasure can teach us about life across the British Empire and the world's trading routes from Europe to America, Asia and perhaps even beyond, from the sixteenth to the eighteenth centuries, this discovery is priceless indeed.

Turn to page ten for our detailed report on the expedition to discover the 'not-Oak Island' treasure. See page twelve for speculation as to the identity of the anonymous, altruistic informant.

❊ ❊ ❊

If you have enjoyed this book, please visit **www.sophiaslewfoot.co.uk** to find out more!

From the website you can sign up to receive news and notifications of forthcoming Sophia Slewfoot Solves History's Mysteries books and you can follow Sophia Slewfoot on social media (Twitter @SSlewfoot; Instagram sophiaslewfoot).

History fan Sophia Slewfoot is a budding amateur detective who loves nothing more than curling up with a good whodunnit or, even better, finding a real life mystery to unravel. Join Sophia, her best friend Betty and her beloved Beagle Toby, as they embark on amazing adventures to solve some of the many mysteries which, throughout history and even to this day, have otherwise remained unexplained...

The Ghost Ship Mary Celeste

What happened to the Victorian ghost ship, the Mary Celeste? Was it magic or malevolence of some kind which caused the crew to disappear? Can Sophia solve the mystery that has baffled some of the world's greatest minds over the last century? Can she somehow even save the day?!

Delve into myth, legend, fact and more than a little fiction, to accompany Sophia on the very first of her history's mystery-solving missions.

Shergar the Stolen Stallion

Sophia and her best friend Betty Babbington have found themselves embroiled in a shocking mystery which combines their love of history with their passion for all things horse riding-related.

What happened to Shergar? How did he disappear, as if into thin air? Can Sophia and Betty solve the mystery that rocked the racing world and baffled the police, international investigators and the world's media? Can they even discover (and rescue?!) the magnificent racing champion?!

Delve into myth, legend, fact and more than a little fiction, to accompany Sophia and Betty on a fast-paced, perilous history's mystery-solving mission.

 pecial Edition, in association with
Crieff Hydro Hotel & Resort:

Crieff Hydro's White Lady

Who was the Crieff Hydro White Lady? Where did she come from? When did she come from? Was she good or was she evil? Does she still roam the hotel?!

Delve into myth, legend, fact and more than a little fiction, to accompany Sophia on a very special, one-off history's mystery-solving mission based at an exceptional, historical, Scottish family resort.